SHADOWED BY SIN

A GOTHIC ROMANCE

Layna Pimentel

Romance At Large Publishing

Romance At Large Publishing
lhautanen@shaw.ca

Publisher's Note: This is a work of fiction. Names, characters, places, and incidents are a product of the author's imagination. Locales and public names are sometimes used for atmospheric purposes. Any resemblance to actual people, living or dead, or to businesses, companies, events, institutions, or locales is completely coincidental.

Book Layout ©2013 BookDesignTemplates.com
Cover Art ©2015 Dar Albert
Edited by JoAnne Soper-Cook

Shadowed By Sin / Layna Pimentel. -- 1st ed.
ISBN 978-0-9937307-7-1

Dedication

Felicity and Savannah, I love you more than words can describe. Your dreams are always within reach. Just remember to never give up.

I'll tell you ... what real love is. It is blind devotion, unquestioning self-humiliation, utter submission, trust and belief against yourself and against the whole world, giving up your whole heart and soul to the smiter -- as I did!

— CHARLES DICKENS, *Great Expectations*

CHAPTER ONE

Benedict St. John glared ice-cold daggers at his father. The marquess paced behind his desk, muttering oaths and, within his meaty grip, he held a crumpled piece of paper. Benedict didn't know what had the patriarch so vexed, however, whatever it was, had to have been infuriating enough to radiate contempt. To have pulled him away from making arrangements for his and Estelle's wedding had to have been of great importance.

Exhaling, Benedict took a seat by the fireplace, but not before reaching for the brandy his father left out on the sideboard. He swirled the amber liquid and inhaled the sweet scent of the indulgence; the liquor his father preferred to drink when something went awry.

"Dare I ask what has you in such a state, Father?"

"I'm not sure if you want to be privy to such information. It's a bloody scandal. Your mother is going to be surly when she finds out. Not to mention how the rest of our family will be dragged through the mud. No, it is crucial we put a stop to this madness."

Benedict winced, knowing all too well his mother would only give her scathing disapproval if the situation were related to their finances. They had led a comfortable lifestyle up until now and, while taking up a smaller residence wouldn't bother him that much, his mother would certainly object. He imagined his mother's words spewing and sputtering, *society this, and society that.* They would be ruined, and she would be too embarrassed to face society. She would insist that they leave town, and God would only know to where.

In fact, while he maintained a small income and the inheritance he received from his grandfather, the time had arrived for him to consider moving into his own residence. Something he should have done some time ago, but his resolve in ensuring him and Estelle had enough income without relying heavily on his parents had weighed on him greatly.

With his nuptials to Lady Estelle Humphrey pending, he really should have established their family residence by now. He had no excuse to not have it completed already. Their wedding being more than a month away certainly didn't leave him more time to piss about and squander time he didn't have.

"Father, come and sit down with me. I am certain we can discern how much trouble the family is in. If there is an opportunity to consolidate properties—"

The earl guffawed at the suggestion. "My dear boy; let me ascertain that none of the servants are nearby and I will confide in you. What I have to say impacts on everyone and I want to make sure this information stays between you and me."

Benedict raised a brow at his father's comment. What on earth, could the man be hiding?

His father joined him seconds later after locking the library door behind him, and poured himself a dram of brandy. He dropped into his seat after downing the alcohol and closed his eyes.

"A few months ago, during one of Cuthbert's famous games he hosted at Crockford's, he won a most exclusive prize. I was present for the game but nothing more. I left shortly after the win and headed home. I will not name names, but the possessions that were to be turned over never happened. One night I stumbled across a most unsettling scene at the Seven Dials."

Benedict sat up and pinched the bridge of his nose and winced. "Just what in the world were you doing at the Seven Dials, Father?"

"My presence there is not of your concern, however, this bleeding demand is."

His father tossed the crumpled missive into his lap. Benedict inspected the parchment, immediately recognizing the insignia at the bottom of the velum. The Earl of Hawthorne's seal couldn't be ignored. But what could the man have written to gain his father's disdain? Benedict unraveled the mess and read on.

Lord St. John,

It should come as no surprise that you are receiving this note. After all, you will be considered an accomplice should the inspector come sniffing at your heels. It would be in your best interest to never remember the events of last midsummer's eve. Furthermore, I also would like to ask that you look into taking care of a particular problem for me. Consider this your last act of loyalty to me and my family. Should that not be enough, ponder what will happen if you don't.

I have it on good authority that French investigators will be landing any day now. I would like for you to secure information as to the nature of their visit. I know of your connections to certain inspectors, and I know that they've come to you in the past. Collect as much information as you can, and I will send word for when we shall meet in private in a fortnight.

Regards,

Lord Cuthbert, 5th Earl of Hawthorne

Benedict relaxed back in his seat, searching his soul for the right words and praying to the good Lord for patience. The note implied his father witnessed a crime he should not have, but precisely what exactly eluded him.

After a few silent moments, Benedict rose from his seat, crossing the floor to stand next to a bookcase. He leaned his shoulder against the hardwood casing, fingered the intricate etchings and inhaled sharply. None of the scenarios playing in his mind ended well. If his father could solve an unsolved mystery, he should do the honorable thing by contacting the authorities. However, the threat of their family being in danger certainly put them at risk.

"What exactly could the Earl of Hawthorne hold against you, Father?"

"I might have had a hand in some cheating at cards; or I might have some information on fugitives from the law."

Benedict groaned loudly. He didn't think his father was capable of retaining such knowledge, let alone being an accessory to unlawful mischief.

"Father, I need a full account of what exactly you saw, and how much you know. I will not allow our family to be dragged through the gossip rags because of some infidelity or illegal gambling."

The earl sighed. "If only it were that simple, my son."

"Then simplify the situation. I want to help you, but I cannot if I do not understand the severity of the situation. I need names, and our associations. If Lord Cuthbert is keeping poor company, I forbid you from any further contact with him." His father, bereft of speech, stared at him with an empty gaze.

"I ask you again, Father. What does he hold over you? What did you witness that you shouldn't have?"

"I stumbled across his henchmen executing the man who failed to pay up his debt from the card game. He was found in the Thames a week later but the Met haven't been able to solve the murder. They've apparently launched a full-fledged investigation led by their head inspector. Is it any wonder he has not been discovered yet?"

His father paused with a notable sigh, poured himself another drink and continued. "With George returning to the continent early, one can only surmise he has found himself in trouble."

"What kind of trouble do you suppose? I shudder to think he's done worse than his father; however, if the French are on their way to possibly apprehend a criminal, well now, that certainly makes things even more interesting. If I don't help him, I'll be an accessory to the murder I witnessed and goodness only knows what atrocity he will set up against me. Don't you see?" He exhaled heavily. "I have to do this for him. If I don't, think of what this will do to you and your mother."

Now it was Benedict's turn to pace the library. *There has to be a way to gain more information about how deep Lord Cuthbert's affiliation with the criminal activity went,* he pondered silently. Nerves racked his core, leaving his throat dry and his temples throbbing. He certainly didn't need this kind of trouble before his wedding. Perhaps a few hours searching for a home would provide him with the silence he needed to contemplate their next actions.

He glared at the crumpled paper and began to fold it as neatly as possible.

"What are you doing with that, Benedict?"

"I am keeping this paper before you do anything more foolish. Do not say or do anything else. I will ascertain how much the man could frame you for, and will decide how we proceed. There's too much at stake and I will not risk dragging Estelle's family into this either."

They were interrupted when a quick knock at the door distracted them. Benedict strode to the door in three giant strides and unlocked it.

A servant bowed and stepped in. "Pardon the intrusion, my lords. This just arrived for Master Benedict."

The butler passed him an envelope with the identical wax seal from the note his father received earlier. Only this time, the letter was decorated with intricate designs.

"Thank you, Horace."

"What is it? Who is it from?" his father asked quizzically.

"I don't know, Father. I'll have a look at it later. I'm rather late for a few appointments now. I will check in on you later this afternoon. Do tell Mother I will be asking Estelle to join us for dinner tonight."

His father groaned yet again. While his parents approved of his desire to marry, they simply did not care for his selection of a wife. The aristocratic snobs that they were, they had expected him to marry an equal, or a lady that came with an extremely large dowry. Estelle was Baron Humphrey's daughter, and while her dowry wasn't that of an earl's or viscount's daughter, her purse strings and entitlements didn't bother him in the least.

From the moment he saw her for the first time at the market, he'd been smitten with the petite and exotic beauty. He'd lifted her from the muddy street, and as her deep dark eyes settled on his, she'd bewitched him. Mind, it took several weeks for him to dissuade another potential suitor, not that the lad stood a chance. Estelle was one catch he would never give up, and now he had to find the perfect home for them, but where? She lived in town with her father and widowed aunt in a modest townhouse during the season, and after that, they resided in a country home with a full set of staff and several tenants to oversee. All of which he could match with his inheritance; but for Estelle everything had to be perfect. She deserved nothing but the world, and if he could give it to her, he would.

"Horace," Benedict called out, reaching for his hat. "See that my carriage is ready post haste. I have to go to town and begin looking at properties."

"Yes, my lord. Right away." The butler disappeared around the corner, leaving Benedict alone in the foyer.

He desperately wanted to open the envelope but refused to do it so close to home. He didn't want his father to worry, nor did he want the servants to speculate on what was the matter. He'd open the blasted thing and read it in the privacy of his carriage.

Darkness shrouded the street, as if evil lurked for its first victim of the day. He stepped in, and gave his driver directions to Mayfair. A quick scout of the area would give him an idea of where there might be some opportunities. His future countess deserved the best. After scouring some neighborhoods, he'd collect his lovely bride and return home for dinner.

A few minutes into the drive, he pulled out the letter and opened it.

Lord Benedict St. John,

You are formally invited to Hawthorne Hall as a guest of Lord George Cuthbert. Celebrations are expected to last a week, and we hope that you will stay for the duration. Several festivities, including a masque, will be held in honor of George's return from the continent. We hope you will attend, and look forward to being introduced to your lovely bride-to-be.

Regards,

Lady Cuthbert, Countess of Hawthorne.

Nothing made sense. Why would Lord Cuthbert send a letter blackmailing his father, and then invite him and Estelle to attend a party at Hawthorne Hall? It had to be a ruse of sorts, but then again, he could use this as an opportunity to dig more into the situation with his father. Yet, was it wise to introduce Estelle to this particular crowd of society, especially when there were other sinister things being plotted? If anything happened to Estelle while she was in his protection, he would never forgive himself. Nevertheless, if he told her about his plan and what was happening, she might be willing to aid him in freeing his father from the devil's clutches. Lord…what was he to do? He needed time but unfortunately he didn't have any. His father only had a fortnight before his private meeting with Cuthbert.

He scanned the streets of Mayfair and found nothing of interest. But, of course, he should probably also include Estelle in the house-hunting too. He'd discuss it with her when he picked her up. Benedict knocked on the window. "Take me to Lord Humphrey's townhouse. I think it is high time I pick up Estelle."

The carriage turned around, exposing the sky growing darker by the second. Tonight he would formulate a plan, and in no time they'd be free from the clutches of a crooked aristocrat.

Twenty minutes later, he arrived at Estelle's doorstep, pondering if he should even tell her at all about the invitation. He really should; after all, she'd notice if he began to behave peculiarly, or noticed him disappearing to take advantage of an empty library or such. It was settled then. He would inform her of his plan, but only within the privacy of his carriage on the way to dinner.

Benedict had barely stepped out when the Humphrey's butler opened the door. "My lord, you are here quite unexpectedly. Come in before the downpour begins."

He hadn't been present in the hallway for a minute when Baron Humphrey came out to greet him. "My dear fellow, I was hoping you would stop by soon. I wanted to discuss with you some of my own plans for the wedding. Follow me, and we will have a brandy before I summon Estelle down."

Benedict raised a speculative brow, but nevertheless smiled at his future father-inlaw's request. He glanced about the parlor, observing the finer nuances of the small room; fine furniture, intricate and ornate woodwork on the fireplace mantle. The townhouse was deemed comfortable for a small family. Just how on earth would Estelle react to being placed in a large household without having ever run one before? It was clear their transition would have to be a slow one. He'd certainly consult with her on her desires for the neighborhood, decor and staff. Ultimately he wanted her happy and would do anything to keep in her good graces.

Baron Humphrey extended his hand to his future son-in-law. "Lord St. John—"

"I've already told you, we are family. Please, call me Ben."

"Very well, Benedict. Here is my plan. I know that you expressed a desire in taking my only daughter on a honeymoon but the girl seems to think you needn't spend a fortune on one. My sister and I wish to contribute funds toward the trip. We have secured a passage for you and Estelle on a tour of the continent."

Pride swelled in his chest to know that the baron truly loved his daughter enough to contribute in such a manner. He could picture her face though. She'd certainly be cross, but who was he to deny her father's wish?

"While that sounds wonderful, Lord Humphrey, what will Estelle think on the subject?"

"That, my son, matters not. The both of you will already be preoccupied by the preparations of the necessities, so this is our gift to you."

Benedict couldn't argue with the man, but he dared not think on what his lovely fiancée would have to say on the arrangement.

"I accept and you have my gratitude, Lord Humphrey. I was wondering if perchance I could steal away my lovely fiancée for dinner tonight."

"Absolutely. I imagine she would not mind one bit in breaking away for a little while. Where will you be dining this evening?"

"With my parents, of course."

"Perfect. William!" the baron shouted out to his butler. "See that Estelle is ready to depart. She shan't keep the earl waiting." Lord Humphrey returned his attention to Benedict and asked, "Have you found a home yet for the both of you?"

"No, I have not. I was hoping to get some idea of where Estelle wanted to live. Sir, not to get off topic, but have you heard the gossip about that body they found floating in the Thames last summer?"

The baron pulled off his spectacles and covered his light cough with a handkerchief. "I have, but it is hard to say how much is fact or fiction. Some of my associates seem to think there is more to the story other than the gent being in the wrong place at the wrong time."

"How so?" Benedict asked, hoping that any speculation would lean toward the Earl of Hawthorne.

"Well, the gent, they say, usually gambled with the higher echelons of the aristocracy. Some have heard the rumors he recently lost several horses and the deed to a rather large estate to Lord Cuthbert, but there is no evidence to support the suspicions. I suppose we may never know the truth of the matter. Anything that could shed some light on the case has probably drifted off to the North Sea. Pity that. I've heard some nasty words mentioned about Cuthbert too."

A sinking feeling burrowed deeper and deeper into Benedict's belly about the earl. How was it even remotely possible for the man to create so much havoc and not leave a trace of his actions behind? There was only one type of man capable of such chaos and deception, and heaven forbid if he'd created strife over his ruling at Hawthorne Hall. If there were one case, there would certainly be others and if that was the scenario, how many other secrets about the family's history was questionable?

Aware someone had joined them, a delightful figure appeared at the parlor door. Estelle curtseyed, acknowledging her father and then Ben.

"I thought you could join my family for dinner tonight." Benedict turned to face the baron. "I will return your lovely daughter just as soon as post dinner refreshments have completed."

"Thank you, son. You two have a wonderful evening while I try and figure out what my sister, Mrs. Black, is planning for the rest of the night. Lord only knows she's got some kind of tea and gossip party to attend."

CHAPTER TWO

Estelle smiled warmly at her fiancé, counting the days in her head before they were married, before turning her head to look out the window.

"I've missed you, dearest. I wondered what was taking you so long but then I saw the weather was turning so I imagined you held off on coming until you knew the weather would cooperate," Estelle said in a soft voice.

Benedict squeezed her hand and lifted her onto his lap. She twisted so that she could kiss him only now; he slid her from his lap so that her back lay flat on their seat. His lips crushed to hers in one swoop. Estelle couldn't think with all her emotions rising to the surface.

"Lord, I cannot wait for our special day," Benedict grumbled, viciously prying away from her.

A giggle escaped her lips as she propped herself up. "Soon enough, my darling, soon enough."

"Let us right your hair before I get a sound thrashing from my mother if you appear in such a state."

"Not to worry, my love, I'll set everything right. What were you and my father discussing when you arrived? It almost felt as if I interrupted something important."

He raised a brow at her question then eased back into his seat. "Aside from wedding plans, we were discussing real estate, and current affairs."

"The current affairs part sounds dreadfully boring. That is, unless, you are referring to something positively scandalous. Has there been a murder? Corruption from the House of Lords; how about some industry about to meet financial ruin?"

"Slow down, my love. It almost sounds as if you have been keeping yourself occupied with current gossip and news. What would you know of financial ruin or murder? Have you heard of something that I have not?"

"Did you not hear about the man floating in the bloody river a few months ago?" Hell, she'd surprised herself with the language, but she doubted Benedict would comment on her choice of words.

"Yes, I heard. In fact, I only just found out about it this afternoon."

"The details around the death are sketchy. They have no suspects, and it's supposed whoever the vagabond is, has probably retreated from London by now."

"Suppose it wasn't a vagabond, and it was a peer?"

"Now that would truly be a scandal, Ben. Do you think it was a member of one of those clubs I hear Papa discussing with guests? There are always those kinds of deals going on. At least that is what I've gathered from my eavesdropping, which I am aware is terribly wrong and ill-mannered, but sometimes there really isn't anything to do at night besides reading. Drat. Ben, what am I to do with these thoughts of intrigue and murder?"

Ben sighed, as he always did when he grew weary of her questions, although, he raised a brow at her mention of eavesdropping.

"I apologize if I'm being a bother. I'll say no more on the matter," Estelle added with a frown.

"It's not that, Estelle. Here, I want you to read this and tell me your thoughts."

Estelle took the invitation and read it. *Why in the world did the words Cuthbert and Hawthorne Hall sound so familiar? Cuthbert…who do I know with that name?*

"So…do you think you want to attend?" he asked.

"I suppose, but do you know them?"

"I went to university with their son George, and at best he was only an acquaintance. Our affiliation ended there. However, there's a matter of the other things I've heard over the years. Estelle, the reason I bring this up now is because there's a bit of a complication with this trip."

He paused and then turned his head away from her.

Estelle couldn't understand why he seemed so worried. "What sort of complication, Ben? You're worrying me."

"There was a letter sent to my father today by the Earl of Hawthorne. He's being blackmailed after witnessing something he shouldn't have and if he does not come into information within a fortnight, he will be framed as the murderer of the man found floating down the river."

Estelle hadn't meant to gasp so loudly but finding the courage not to was even more difficult.

"You cannot be serious. Blackmail. How absurd! But why?"

"I do not know for certain; but all I know is that my father would never do anything to jeopardize his family in the least. The Earl of Hawthorne is up to no good and I will not tolerate his interference, which leads to my next question. If we go to this masque or whatever the Countess of Hawthorne wants to address it as, I may drift away from your side. It is my intention to use that opportunity to investigate from within the earl's home. I hope you will agree with what I intend to do, but would certainly understand if you wish to decline the invitation."

"I refuse to bow out. We are in this together, Benedict. Our families will become one soon enough that we must learn to work together. If there is anything I can do to aid you, I want to help."

"I thank you for your support, dear, but I do not want to endanger you either. There will be times I must slip away, and when that is the case, I do not want you to follow. Should the earl suspect that I am there for other reasons than his son's entertainment, who knows what they are capable of doing? One man has ended up in the river. How many others have there been and never been found? I do not want you to get that close, and should you ever stumble on anything so horrifying, you are to inform me immediately. The second I know you are no longer safe amongst the guests; you will be on the next coach home." The intensity in his voice wavered and she observed the flurry of emotions crossing his face;

anger, fear, sadness, and rage. She understood the need to protect his family, but at what cost?

I cannot lose him to this, she vowed silently.

Estelle prayed that whatever happened during their stay at Hawthorne Hall, nothing too drastic would occur. Every manor had secrets, and hopefully Benedict wouldn't have to dig too deep to uncover them.

The carriage came to a halt, and a rush of attendants greeted them.

Ben exited first and aided her down, while servants lined up at the door. When they reached the main room, she was greeted by her future mother-in-law, who made it no secret she was still not pleased with their betrothal. In fact, if she had to bet her life on it, she probably had some other doe-eyed debutante picked out for him. Estelle shuddered to think what she might have thought of her the first time, when her son professed his love for her.

"How nice of you to join us, Estelle. Come and sit with me for a bit. Dinner should be ready in a quarter hour. Tell me of your plans so far."

"The plans are coming along nicely, my lady. Although, Benedict seems to be keeping me in suspense with the plans for our new home."

"I'm sure it will be quite lovely. My son is quite adept at procuring oddities, and I'm positive he will find you something fitting."

Her words bit, and with the sting of the insult Estelle only smiled, and was saved by a servant announcing dinner was ready.

Without a second to waste, Benedict fell into step with her on their way to the dining hall. He winked and whispered to her, "I do hope the weather takes a turn for the worst."

She glared at him. His subtle suggestion that they engage in some of their own mischief was terrible, but how she loved him deeply. There wasn't anything she wouldn't do for him. However, if they were caught in the middle of anything inappropriate, the wedding would be cancelled or even moved up. Then where would they live?

Estelle's cheeks heated and she gently shoved him away. "Do stop, you are embarrassing me," she replied with a hoarse whisper.

"If you think that's embarrassing, I would hate to see what happens if I ever told you my fantasies about you."

She smacked him then, and he only laughed at her. They were seated across from each other, as were Benedict's parents. Oddly enough, she noticed the silent signals he and his father exchanged—wary glances, slight coughing, and petty small talk—when his mother spoke up.

"Dare I ask what is left of the wedding planning, you two? You're obviously doing a fine job discussing it discreetly in the corner over there and it has become apparent that neither of you want our assistance, but I am rather put out over the exclusion."

"We meant no offense, Mother. Everything is quite settled with the exception of our future home."

"In that case, I will insist on aiding you both with the hiring of servants. I have already been seeking out names for all the staff you will require. All you will need to do is find the appropriate home for your future. Estelle needs a home befitting that of a countess. You cannot live in a hovel and call it a home. I will provide you with my recommendations for all of the above and you will not procure a home unless I approve all manners of its state."

Estelle dropped her spoon at the countess's tone. Of all the condescending, pigheaded, arrogant things the woman could say, she dared to interfere in the manner of what residence was selected.

"How generous of you, my lady. However I was thinking that Benedict and I could stay at the hotel until we have returned from our honeymoon. I do believe we will be going away for a time, so I would hate to rush things at this point."

The countess snorted in an unladylike manner. Lord St. John's eyes narrowed, and her gaze shifted between them. "Well, it would appear I've lost my appetite."

Her mother-in-law rose from the table and re-treated from the dining hall like a wounded animal.

"Oh, ignore her. She still hasn't forgotten over her proposals you previously rejected for prospective brides. I mean no offense to you of course, Lady Estelle. My wife has been accustomed all these years to getting her way, and now she feels as if she needs to prove herself more worthy of her title and defend it. Lord only knows why," Lord St. John drawled before tossing his napkin on the table.

A crack of lightning and thunder rattled around them. Rain pelted against the windows, making a frightening sound. Estelle raised her head to only find Benedict smiling.

"I guess this means you will be spending the night here, my love."

"Indeed," his father added. "Shall we move into the library and sit by the fire a while? I think a dram of brandy shall settle our nerves. It has been quite the exhausting day."

Left alone in the library, Benedict flagged his father's attention. "Father, I have a plan."

Lord St. John paled, noticing Estelle watching them intently. He probably hadn't expected for his son to share the information given the circumstances, but he hoped he would overlook that oversight.

"Do not worry about Estelle. I've told her everything and I trust that she won't breathe a word of this to one living soul. We, meaning Estelle and I, received an invitation earlier today to attend Hawthorne Hall. The earl and his countess are hosting a masque in celebration of George's return from the continent. This will provide me with the greatest opportunity to delve deeper into anything else Lord Cuthbert may be hiding."

"You cannot mean to thrust your intended into the middle of this mess? It's dangerous, Benedict. You don't know what that man is capable of, and I could not live with myself if anything were to happen to Estelle."

"Nothing will happen to me, my lord. Benedict will be there to protect me, and should anything go awry, I will be on the next coach headed home. Besides, I am certain my aunt will feel obligated to serve as my chaperone." Estelle rose from her seat in an attempt to settle his nerves, but he lifted his hand to stop her.

"You do realize if we're all found out, there will be dire consequences." Estelle nodded, as did his son.

"Very well, I do not want to hear any more of this plan. Estelle, I will see that one of the maids tends to you for the remainder of the evening if that will suit."

"That would be appreciated, my lord." Lord St. John quickly left the room.

Perhaps going to the masque is a mistake, she thought.

The storm outside refused to relent, and the thrashing sounds of tree branches whipping around in the frightening atmosphere outside, kept making a clatter, hitting one of the smaller buildings on the property. Estelle loathed storms, especially when she wasn't at home in the cozy town residence her father kept after her mother passed on. Staying on for the night in Benedict's family home might prove to be a challenge after all.

"If I didn't know any better, Estelle, I'd say you look frightened. Come here," Benedict coaxed, trying to pull her into an embrace.

Estelle complied, feeling insecure. Butterflies in her belly fluttered, as uncertainty washed over her. How she loved this man, even if the way they met was unconventional and his family didn't approve. He complemented her like lace on a bonnet, and to think they would serve a lifetime in holy matrimony in just a few short weeks.

"Ben, I should probably get to bed as I will need to leave early. My father will wonder why—"

"Do not worry about a thing. Your father and aunt will understand that the weather was not acceptable to travel in. Besides, if you are worried that I will compromise you in any way, I wouldn't do anything unless you wanted me to."

"It isn't that. It's everything else. Your father appeared truly dismayed that you had informed me of what has already transpired. For heaven's sake, the man looked like he was going to swoon like a woman."

"Yes, but that is only because there isn't anything he would not do to protect us either. Nevertheless, I will not stand by idly waiting for him to take the blame for something he had no part in. We will get to the bottom of this. Ah, I believe I hear your maid coming along. Go on up with her and I will stop in and see you once the whole house has turned down for the evening."

Estelle nodded and watched the parlor door open slowly. The glow of the candle the maid held cast frightful shadows against the wall.

"I'll be tending to your needs tonight, Lady Estelle, if you will follow me. It did take me some time to find a nightgown that will suit you for the night. We will have your clothing laundered tonight as well. Everything should be nice and dry for you by morning."

"Thank you kindly."

They entered her bedroom for the night, making quick work of changing into a clean and modest night rail. A yawn escaped her lips as she stretched after sitting down at the edge of the bed. Her maid left her with a single candle burning, and a low fire that barely kept the room warm. She wondered if Benedict had any intentions of spending the night with her, or if he'd simply stop in to wish her well before bed.

She collapsed back and stared into the darkness above her, remembering how they'd played in the carriage on their way here. She wasn't exactly obtuse with the way men viewed and wanted women. Her education—if one could call it that—came from the fanciful novels her aunt hid in her papa's library. Mind, they weren't for her virginal reading pleasure, but what her aunt didn't know, wouldn't send her into an apoplectic fit.

A quiet rap at the door strayed her from her thoughts.

"I wanted to see how you were getting along. I promise not to keep you too long." He locked the door behind him and sat next to her on the bed.

Excitement welled up deep within her chest, and when he was this close to her, she had never felt safer in her entire life. Estelle sighed and whispered, "Ben, kiss me please."

"I think I can accommodate that request." He bent forward, capturing her lips, slowly ravaging her mouth. Her heart hammered in her chest, and she was gently coaxed to lie back on the bed. His one hand slid in behind her head, cradling the base of her skull. Every swipe of his tongue delved deeper and deeper, bringing her toward an unknown feeling of rapture. They'd shared many tender kisses, embracing until their privacy was infringed upon by her father, passers-by, or by the sheer stupidity of knocking a chair over. Yet, in this moment, everything shone in a new light. This man would be her husband, and she'd have a lifetime of these small pleasures. She quivered beneath his expert caresses, giving in to the wanton sensation fluttering about in her belly, clouding her sensibility of how they acted without decorum.

Estelle shifted her legs apart as the man she loved eased himself between them, lying atop her and delighting her with a slow need. She burned for him. He lifted her nightgown, leaving her thighs exposed to the cooling air in her chambers. A shiver crept up her spine and goose flesh swept across her legs. Lord, how the man drove her out of her wits.

The sound of feet shuffling down the hall brought her awareness to the present. She pressed her palms against Benedict's chest and whispered, "We need to stop. Your parents cannot find us in this compromising state."

He kissed her hard, robbing her of any further thought and then he stopped, slowly easing himself off her. "Very well, my love. Until tomorrow; and I trust you will have pleasant dreams."

Estelle bit her lower lip as she watched him walk away. *Only a few more weeks until we are married, darling.*

CHAPTER THREE

"I will avenge you, dear Helen. Just you wait and see." Edwin Cuthbert locked the secret passageway leading from his sister's old room. The dank smell of mold and mildew in his uncle's manor made the river-rock walls slick with slime. The decayed flesh of rodents littered the floor. Cobwebs hung loosely near the rooms he frequented, and while they would normally upset the fairer sex, he found their presence pleasant.

When he learned of his uncle's decision to host a masquerade in honor of his son's return from the continent, betrayal beat fervently in his chest, leading him directly to Helen's room. *How I miss her so.* Not only did the fool invite the very man who had once associated with his cousin, George, but also it'd been George himself who led poor Helen to her death. Were it not for him she would have never insisted on departing to the country. Coming to her room offered him comfort in times of helplessness.

Never mind the issue that the very woman who had cut him down was due to arrive at any time today with her fiancé. He desired to speak with her during the snobbish event, and perhaps find a way to lure her away from this place. The masquerade ball would provide him the proper cover he required to get her to slip away undetected. However, the only question that remained was, how could he convince her to leave? If she lingered at Hawthorne Hall, George would likely find a way to scandalize her, and he could never allow it to happen.

Edwin could not comprehend, nor find the necessity in the extravagant show being held to honor a son who had never worked hard in his life, and on the anniversary of the day his sister departed this realm most suspiciously. While society and the gossip rags all speculated—to some degree—that he had his hand in the death, only he knew the truth. To lift a hand and cause harm to his sister was a deplorable and idiotic notion. Edwin seethed with fury. Blind with rage, he pounded on the walls of the passage. "I will end it all. Make no mistake."

He tried to control his anger yet reality swallowed him whole. Despair over losing everything he had ever loved gripped his heart. The entire family would soon be exposed for the true shams they were. The Earl of Hawthorne's crimes would be uncovered soon enough. How his uncle's shady dealings had not been caught astounded him profoundly. If only the investigators had looked deeper into the deaths of those men found in the Thames. George would pay dearly for his indiscretions, and his aunt, the countess, would forever burn in purgatory. Her sins would earn her that special place in the Devil's arms.

He reached the end of the corridor that opened to the servants' wing. Edwin swung a flap of fabric to reveal the empty hallway.

Edwin smirked reaching for the latch, and quietly stepped out into the hall. Checking his pocket watch, he noted he had enough time to descend the stairs to his quarters before anyone would notice.

Next week the games begin. Edwin unlatched the panel and slipped down the hall toward the service stairs the servants used, but stopped when someone whispered his name harshly from the steps leading from the attic.

"What in God's name are you doing here, Master Edwin? Trying to get into the attic like your cousin George?"

"I beg your pardon? George came up this way? How long ago?"

"Indeed, and I am going to tell you exactly what I told him. Be gone from this wing. There is nothing here for you boys."

"We are not boys. We are men. The sooner you understand, Evan, the better things will be. Last I recall you are in no position to be telling me where I can, or cannot go."

"Never you mind. Run along, and do not let me see you this way again, or I will be telling the earl."

Edwin scoffed over Evan's, the first footman's, warning. If that man was not careful of the threats he tossed about, he would end up dead too. Danger hung like a black cloud here at Hawthorne Hall, but it was not him. While there were those who would speculate his comings and goings, he could not take the entirety of the credit for the worry and fear clenching around people's hearts. A fear so deep and hideous, it was like the serpent of Eden coiling around the organ, squeezing the life out of its victim at the behest of its commanding lord. A demon that lusted after possessions that did not belong to him lurked these halls, planning and coveting things and people in unconventional and devious ways; a

lecherous fool whose sole purpose in this exist-
ence tormented Edwin at every turn.

Every damned secret this house holds would
be exposed before he bore his last breath.

It is the best I can do, my dear Helen.

On his way to his room, Edwin detoured and
wandered to the main floor where he happened
across a whispered conversation between his uncle and another unfamiliar voice. He glanced
around to ensure no one discovered his eavesdropping.

"I've just received word; Lord St. John's son
will be attending the masque with his fiancée.
Find out everything you can about Baron Humphrey. I need leverage, damn it!"

"What if St. John doesn't provide you with the
information you are seeking?"

"Then we use both his son and future daugh-
ter-in-law. I cannot have that man interfering with
my plans and I will not take blame for anything. It
is out of the question!"

"You don't mean to—"

"What? Kill them? Only if necessary. What part
of 'I will not be held accountable for the misdeeds
and dishonesty of others' do you not understand?
St. John was given a task and should he not
complete it, if I need to kill the boy or the girl, I

will. Now go and do what I've paid you to do. Remember, absolute discretion. I cannot have you falter along the way."

Just what is the old goat up to now? Did he mean to do away with Estelle? They practically killed his sister, and like hell was he going to allow him to kill the only other woman he'd cared for.

Edwin rushed to his room, ignoring any servants he passed. He must send a note to Estelle immediately and warn her not to come. He had to do something. This is the only way.

His cousin burst through as cantankerous as ever. The bugger had always found a way to get under his skin, and today would be no different.

"What are you doing? Writing yourself a love note like those foolish poets women seem to fawn over these days?"

Edwin rolled his eyes, refraining himself from stooping to the level of his cousin.

While this whole house was convinced that he was troubled, the fact of the matter was this entire manor and its occupants deserved to be in Bedlam or Newgate.

"I am jotting down some notes if you must know. There are things I do not want to forget, and writing them down helps me."

"Well, in the event no one has told you, the masque is full on, and everyone who was invited has accepted. There will be a full house of guests to entertain me. Shall we place a bet as to how many hearts I can break?"

Edwin clenched his fist at his side, ascertaining that this ball was nothing more than a whim for his cousin to torment the guests.

"Who, by chance, was invited, George?"

"Several university mates, the fiancée of one of them, and other peers mother and father deemed suitable. Father is looking to gain some favor over a business prospect so I imagine he is using the affair as an opportunity to win them over. On that note, I will leave you to return to your writing or whatever it is that you're doing, but I should warn you, I want you nowhere near the guests at my party."

"Need I remind you, cousin, I live here too and so did my sister Helen, until you ruined her." He paused, and clucked his tongue while his cousin scowled. "You didn't think I knew about you visiting her, did you? You will rue the day you were born."

His cousin laughed, trying to recompose himself. "You know nothing, and never will. You're nothing but an orphan, and so was your sister.

Oh, and she's dead, and it's only a matter of time before you are too. Hell! The only reason my pa took you in was because of the money that was left behind. You don't honestly think my parents actually love you, do you?"

George sauntered out of his room taking care to slam the door behind him. The action shook the wall and Edwin's night table, knocking a burnt-out candle onto the floor.

Edwin sighed, closing his eyes, imagining the terror that would wreak this house in the days to come. He had visions of married women being seduced by his lecherous cousin; to his uncle bamboozling members of the peerage in some scheme no less. To the countess, drowning her sorrows, whatever they were, in a daily excess of absinthe and laudanum.

Lord how he tired of this life. Perhaps he would end it, much in the same way he'd done his parents. There wasn't a day that passed where he didn't think of them, and their threats of sending him away. His only regret was that Helen never had a chance to say goodbye, but then she was taken so early, too.

Soon enough their awkward family would be reunited.

* * * *

Estelle Humphrey clenched her fists at her sides. *Why did the name on the invitation seem familiar?* She pushed the thought aside, and tried to focus on her and Benedict. Since the announcement of this impromptu trip and the troubles his family had encountered, he'd been distant and troubled.

From the day he'd rescued her from Edwin's persistence on the street corner, they had been inseparable. Who knew that tripping in a mud-coated street would neatly plant her at the feet of the man she was meant to marry? Stolen kisses in the parlor, to her batting off his wandering hands while they strolled along the edges of her father's country estate—she sensed from the very moment they met, their attraction to each other could not be denied. Yet, her body warned her of the dangers of being with a man she hardly knew.

When Benedict approached her father for her hand in marriage, she'd found the proposal a hasty one. But how could she deny the handsome devil that Benedict St. John was? Perhaps during their stay away she would find some privacy with him, discovering his secrets without the hovering shadow of her papa, and Aunt Margaret. Her desire to know more about his family and their connections to the Earl of Hawthorne would certainly break his frigidness. Her father let it slip one Sunday morning after church that Benedict inherited quite a fortune from his grandfather's estate, which didn't include what he stood to inherit when his own father passed. Estelle attempted to bring up the subject, yet her fiancé declined to speak further on the matter. However, the niggling matter of the history of Benedict's father's dealings haunted her. A vise gripped around her heart as uncertainty flooded through her.

He cannot be so horrible, can he? Ben has always been so kind and gentle toward me and my family. He has other amiable traits that surely stand to his credit and his father has always been pleasant. This blackmailing incident is all a misunderstanding.

Estelle closed her eyes, and then gasped. A vision of a darkened cellar and blood dripping down a wall plagued her mind. Sickness washed over her, and she rushed to cover her mouth with her handkerchief.

"Where did you say we are going, Ben?" she asked with a slight quiver in her throat.

"The Earl of Hawthorne's estate. Estelle, what is the matter with you? Your face has gone grey like death."

Her aunt, who had snored for the entire drive, slowly opened her eyes, scrutinizing as if they had been behaving without proper decorum. She closed her eyes again, snoring unscrupulously.

As the carriage slowed its pace, Benedict reached for Estelle's tight-fisted hands. "Dearest, what has you in such a state?"

Estelle sighed as an overwhelming sense of dread washed over her. "I am not certain, my love. The family name is familiar and I cannot help but wonder why. I am uneasy not knowing what has me so unsure," she lied, desperately trying to gain composure. Visions occasionally came and went, with no specific meaning or attachment to anything immediate. She could barely understand why she received one in this instance, but her curse would eventually reveal its truth.

He patted her knee and moved to sit next to her, pulling her into his arms. "Dearest, when we are married at the end of the month, I imagine we will be in the company of people we may or may not remember. That cannot be what has you so vexed."

Estelle nodded. "No, it is not. I have a bad feeling about this trip. Mock me, if that is your inclination, but I swear it on my dear granny's grave, something terrible is going to happen during our stay."

"*Pshaw*, my dear. I would never mock you. In fact, I greatly esteem your ability to 'follow your instincts,' as us gents say."

Though pleased with Benedict supporting her, nothing vanquished the fear and panic rising. When their ride finally halted and the door swung open, Estelle opened her eyes to spy the portly driver lowering the steps.

"Auntie," Estelle patted her aunt's leg, "we've arrived."

"Lord St. John, allow me to assist you," the driver volunteered.

"There is no need, my good man. Just see to our trunks and ensure they are brought to our respective rooms," Benedict said.

The older gentleman nodded and departed toward the footman to leave his instructions.

Estelle masked a yawn that threatened to make a monstrous and unladylike noise. Lord, how she disliked long carriage rides, visions, and intrigues that placed innocents in peril.

"You look exhausted, my dear. Perhaps we should delay in joining the others tonight and rest before dinner."

"To arrive and not thank our host is most decidedly rude, Ben. I must insist we join the others. I will, however, take a small respite before dinner to refresh myself." Reaching for her reticule she stepped out of the vehicle and allowed the enormity of the estate to swallow her.

The estate had been rebuilt over a period of fifty years, while some of the remnants of the original building were kept when the new additions were made. Malicious rumors circulated amongst Londoners as to how and why so many renovations had to be completed; was it haunted by its previous owners and servants? There was much speculation pertaining to the whispers of secret passages, a haunted family crypt, and a dungeon.

Everyone in London or nearby was not immune to the scathing gossip hounds, and the family's history had been known for its scandals. However, it was not until their host welcomed her at the doors did she remember how she knew the name.

"Welcome, welcome, Lord St. John, Miss Humphrey and my dear Mrs. Black. It has been so long since we last met. I am dreadfully sorry about your husband," the Earl of Hawthorne offered as he bowed his head.

"Thank you kindly, my lord. His passing was quite sudden," her aunt said.

"St. John, I am so glad you accepted my invitation. The countess will be most pleased to finally meet you both." Tall, handsome, and distinguished, the aging Earl of Hawthorne smiled warmly at them, but she knew deep down the lies that lurked beneath the surface. He embraced Benedict whose family knew and worked with the earl on many occasions. Her family's only connection to the Cuthbert's was of similar interests. Her father, being a baron, knew and associated with members of the peerage that were mostly watered down. The men gambled, hunted, and even bought connecting lands together. There had been something altogether different with his approach with Benedict. A falseness or dark cloud loomed about him, casting a negative and eerie air. Lord, how she struggled to make sense of the things she couldn't visibly and readily explain.

"Come, come. I will have Mary show you to your rooms." The earl leaned forward and winked at Estelle. The action didn't escape Benedict's notice either and he pulled her into him and gave her a gentle squeeze of comfort. "The countess insisted that I place you both in different wings, but considering Mrs. Black has joined your party, I assume she is here as your chaperone. I will ensure that your party will be kept together. I will, however, insist that you allow me to designate Mary to attend to your needs, Estelle."

She nodded, hoping to get some rest soon. When they stopped at the bedroom door, a footman was leaving from having put her trunk and valise there.

"I will return in just a minute, Miss Estelle. I will show Lord St. John to his room, which is down the hall."

"Very well." Estelle entered the room, finding herself bereft of speech. Her small bedchamber at home paled in comparison to the enormity of this one; decorated for a female with elegant whites, rose colored accents, and a gold leaf trimmed looking glass. The space appeared to have been vacant for some time. Mystery shrouded the chamber much like an early morning fog after a light rain.

A fire burned low in the hearth, casting shadows on the wall where candles were lit, dancing and flickering with movement.

Estelle explored the paneled walls, admiring the great detail in the etchings, until she came to a beautiful portrait of Helen Cuthbert, the earl's niece who had died mysteriously a year before. She remembered the passing all too well. Helen's brother, Edwin, had also proposed to her shortly before the tragic event. She declined of course, but in his tenacity he would not relent. The boy was dreadfully persistent until Benedict had saved her from his nagging and pestering at the market one day. Her father had banned the boy from calling on her ever again, and then one day it stopped, and she never bothered to inquire after him. Considering he was likely to be present during their stay here, the manor was large enough she'd be able to avoid him.

Estelle stepped away from the wall, stalked toward the vanity, and sat down. She took a cloth, dipped it into the washbasin, and covered her face with it. How she desperately needed to feel refreshed, but decided to close her eyes for only the slightest of seconds. Her mind wandered aimlessly at how her wedding plans were progressing. In exactly one month, she and Ben would finally be together.

All that remained of their preparations was the wedding breakfast and their travel abroad. Ben expressed an interest in them travelling to the Continent, but given the amount of money she had heard it would cost, she had been adamant in delaying such a frivolous expenditure.

She yanked off the towel and stood up to loosen her gown, before her maid arrived to assist with her change of gowns. When she removed her corset and stood in nothing but her chemise and stockings, a strange cool air wafted in the room. The candles flickered hard, and returned to the gentle dance.

How odd is that? This wing cannot be so old to be so drafty.

Estelle looked up to stare into the mirror and wished she had been graced with more feminine curves. A scant later, the looking glass shook. She went over to it, to ensure it would not fall, but the blasted thing had been secured to the wall.

What in damnation is going on?

Before she could comprehend the brevity of the situation, a faded image in the looking glass stared back at her and whispered hauntingly, "Stay away from the walls." *Bloody hell! Helen.*

Estelle looked away from the glass to the portrait, and then back to the mirror. The image whispered the warning again, before dissipating into thin air.

Too distraught, Estelle failed to notice her maid entering the room.

"I see you have already beaten me to the undressing, Miss. Let me help you with your gown."

Estelle nodded, but one look at the young maid had her in tears.

"What is amiss, Estelle? Shall I call for Lord St. John?"

"No, no. I am just seeing things. You see, I am quite exhausted. It has been known for a person to be touched at times of extreme fatigue."

"If you would rather not come down, I am certain his lordship will not mind."

While it was a tempting offer, Estelle did not dream of insulting her hosts. Besides that, she did not care to be confined to her room.

"Mary, do you know much of the estate's history?"

"Only what I have heard from the other servants gossiping."

"What about ghosts?"

"Well, that, Miss, you should know too many unexplained things have happened since I came to work here five years ago. So it would not be a far stretch of the imagination if most of us believed in specters coming back to haunt us on unfinished business if you catch my meaning." *An interesting fact.*

"Most excellent, I do hope that you will share your stories with me, when we are alone again."

"Certainly, Miss. Now, let us get you into a fresh gown for dinner. It is my understanding that all the guests have arrived, and the countess has already rang for dinner to be served within the hour."

Estelle nodded and retrieved a gown from her trunk. *Now, to get on with the evening.* If that was the first strange thing to happen since their arrival, Estelle shuddered to think what would transpire next.

First, she was plagued with a vision of a cellar and blood, and now she received otherworldly advice to stay away from the walls. Estelle shook her head with dismay.

Perhaps coming here was a mistake.

CHAPTER FOUR

"Are you well, my dear?" Benedict asked his fiancée. Her usually rosy complexion had blanched, and her hands slightly trembled as she raised a water goblet to her lips. He suspected exhaustion was the culprit, and considering she had not mentioned any other ailments, Benedict did not overly concern himself.

"I am fine, Ben. Whatever it is shall pass."

"If you are certain, however, if you find yourself in a situation where a physician is required; have your aunt summons me and I will fetch one myself." He squeezed her knee, only to receive a warning glare from her aunt who sat on the other side of her.

She nodded in response and he carried on eating. It had been so long since he had seen his friends and found it immensely convenient and peculiar that all of them were invited to Lord Cuthbert's estate in welcoming his son. At the very least, it would make their stay less dull. The boys at the best of times were well known to be ill-mannered, walking and living demons bent on sin, and brawling. But what young man did not?

He nodded at his friends across the table, and would introduce his lovely wife-to-be to his companions from university. There were times he wondered what the boys had been up to. A few months back he had heard rumors of Camden's money trouble, and his father's scandal with investors.

One never knew what could be trusted in the whispers, but everyone knew an ounce of truth could always be found in rubbish.

"Miss Estelle, how is Baron Humphrey these days?" Lord Cuthbert called out from the end of the table.

Benedict looked at his lovely fiancée, who blushed furiously at the attention. The poor, dear woman disliked being the center of attention.

"Aren't you going to answer him, dearest?"

"My papa is well, Lord Cuthbert. Thank you for inquiring," she said.

"St. John, I would like for you to visit after you and Estelle are wed. I would be honored to host another gathering in your name. I imagine your coffers will be well stocked for years to come."

Benedict nearly choked on his biscuit. "Certainly, my lord. It would be us who would be honored, but we would hate to be any trouble at all. In regards to my financial situation; I assure you my countess will want for nothing, nor will our children."

"Pish-posh. My countess and I would like nothing more. I, for one, think an opportunity such as this is something you should greatly consider."

As the dishes were lifted away from the table, their host and his wife led the party into the ballroom for some music, dancing, and post dinner refreshments.

He led Estelle down the hall when a guest bumped into him, sending Estelle into a table holding a vase.

Benedict grunted from the impact, recovered, and saw to her aid. "Are you hurt?"

"No. I'm fine, Ben. Who bumped into you while rushing down the hall?"

"I have no idea, but once I plant you in a respectable lady's company, I have every intention of discovering who the bastard is."

Now it was her turn to comfort him, and while her touch stirred other emotions than comfort, he did not want to alarm her in any manner.

"Do not fret. I promise not to create any trouble. You are deserving of an apology, and I will ensure you get one."

"Then there is no need to escort me. I will find my own way to the hall, as I am sure I can find my aunt from here." She gritted her teeth and left him in the hall.

What had he said to offend her? He started down the hall in the direction of where the gent headed, but not a single person could be seen; it was almost too quiet, not even a servant. He went to turn around, but the sound of something being thrown against a wall drew him further down the hall until he reached the open door of the library.

A vase lay in a hundred pieces on the floor near a bookcase. *How odd. This doesn't appear to have fallen on its own. Who could have done this?*

Heavy, yet quick steps scurried away from the vicinity, but where to and from? The hairs on the back of his neck stood on end with the possibility that someone had either expected him to follow, or now moved away to watch him with malice. This visit began to grate on his nerves. If things did not improve, they would be leaving tomorrow instead of the weekend.

He followed the corridor leading to the ballroom when he encountered his old friends.

"We were wondering when we would see you again. I daresay, when were you going to tell us of your pending nuptials to that lovely creature that's on the terrace right now?" Camden asked with the dashing smile he often used to charm the ladies.

"I had every intention of doing so this evening. If you follow me, I will see to that matter right away," Benedict said.

"No rush. Come have a drink with us. Duncan is at the table over here. You may join your betrothed momentarily. So, what news do you bring from London? There's been mad gossip about our families."

"Why do you seem so interested in what people have to say, Camden? You weren't much for gossip to begin with."

"No; but seeing as there's been more than one scandal I am interested in learning which one I will have to deal with first. I have only just come back, you see," Camden said.

Yes, he had heard that his friend had gone off to the West Indies. Lord only knew why. Perhaps hiding from debts was what ailed him, gambling what little money he had left, and whoring. In a small way, he was glad that the men had not changed much or he would think them ill, or worst yet, dying.

"Am I correct that I saw Gabriel present?" Benedict asked.

"You are. He left a little while ago to retrieve something from his room. It has been at least a quarter hour; he should be back anytime now."

Gabriel Warren had been the quiet one of the bunch, and very reserved. While he attended most of the men's activities, he rarely took part. Not since Helen.

Wait. Was not Helen the earl's niece?

"Before we join my fiancée, was Gabriel courting the earl's niece?"

Camden rubbed his chin before responding. "Now that you mention it, he did. No wonder the bastard has been unusually quiet tonight."

Benedict could not have imagined how unwelcome his friend would be in the home of a woman he courted.

Henry continued. "Did they ever figure out how she died?"

"No, they did not. In fact, I am certain the authorities suspected her brother, Edwin, but a lack of evidence threw that theory to the wind." Cameron added.

SHADOWED BY SIN | 65

Music from the ballroom spilled out into the side room where they stood. Laughter filled the air while couples moved around them leaving the terrace. He spotted Estelle talking with a few women, including her aunt, before returning his attention to his schoolmates.

"She is quite lovely, St. John. How on earth did you settle on such a creature? I find the notion of you marrying at all quite surprising. How did you meet? How is your father doing?"

Benedict sighed, contemplating how to respond to the question that weighed heavily on his mind as of late. Just how far would the Earl of Hawthorne go to prove a point to his father? While Estelle was not of the higher echelons of the aristocracy, his mother eventually had to come around. For heaven's sake, Estelle would be the mother of his children, his heirs. He cared not for her dowry, for he saved every cent of his inheritance and didn't squander his coin as his friends had over the years. Bah. In the end, all that mattered was that he loved her, and there was not a thing his mother or the Earl of Hawthorne could do to stop them. That is, unless he and Estelle ended up dead.

"I rescued her in the market several months ago from an impertinent pup who followed her about, publicly professing his love for her. She all but tripped into me. Estelle is quite fetching, and I am quite pleased to say that she is mine. As for my father, he is doing as well as can be expected. He doesn't go out much anymore, however my mother takes care of all the socializing at this point."

"By the by, St. John, she will be the prettiest countess these parts have ever laid their eyes upon. Do not be a fool. Don't wait until the end of the month to marry her. Compromise her, and run away to Scotland. I imagine you'll find this gathering much too droll when you could be spending your time more wisely."

He snorted, as did his companions. Benedict swallowed his drink.

A cacophony of shrieking and screaming came from the terrace.

He led the group toward the commotion to find Gabriel's crumpled and lifeless body on the ground. *But how? Did he fall out the window from above?* He lost his breath, and words could not escape his lips even if he tried. His head throbbed as he tried to hold back tears for his friend. He looked up and gazed into Estelle's stoic gaze, and caught her before she swooned.

He dropped to his knees while still holding her. His whole body quaked with fear, sadness, and grief. Benedict squeezed his fiancée one last time before rising to his feet with the aid of Duncan and Henry.

"Do you want me to carry her?" Henry asked mournfully.

Benedict refused to release her. "No, I will carry her myself."

Estelle's aunt fell into step with him, as did their hosts. It was time the evening's festivities ended for the night, and hopefully they could get to the bottom of what happened come morning.

* * * *

Edwin latched the panel closed as quietly as he could from his sister's former fiancé's room. The chamber had been left in a state of disarray. Damn Gabriel for arguing, and damn him for not listening to a word he had to say. His tumble could have been avoided if only he'd tried to understand. *Nothing will ever change*, he reflected. Even from his hiding place within the hidden passages, the shrieking from the terrace echoed all around him, irritating his already throbbing head. He desired nothing more than to gouge his own eyes out. He pinched the bridge of his nose and inhaled sharply, wincing from the pain in his middle from being punched ten minutes earlier.

The assault had been unexpected, but one supposed they had the right to defend themselves. Yet, he should have been prepared and expected the retaliation. *Blast it.*

Edwin needed to return to his room before his uncle noted his absence, but the instant he stepped out of the secret panel in the wall, he heard voices. Pressing against the wall hidden around the corner, he peered to see which guests were approaching when he suddenly spied his cousin watching the guests from the opposite end of the hall.

Lord St. John carried Estelle to her room, with her aunt in tow. The earl followed behind, as did the countess and several servants. Had she swooned? It was then he noticed his cousin slip out of sight, but not before bringing his finger to his lips to order him to keep silent; the audacity his cousin had to command him even from afar. A rush of servants and Estelle's companions left her chambers. Whispers too quiet, he could not hear a syllable from this distance.

If he were to pop into her room and check on her, someone would notice his entry, and would question his sudden interest in her. Her fiancé would decidedly be displeased considering their first encounter a year prior. The only way he could check on her had to be through the passageway, but he could not delay in returning to his room. The earl would check there after the accident to ensure he had not played a part in the tragedy. Yet, one small look in on her could not hurt.

Edwin returned to the secret panel in the hallway and disappeared behind it, desperately trying to make as little noise as possible, until he backed into a nook where he kept a bottle of his aunt's stash of laudanum for the days his head ached. Catching the dusty green bottle, Edwin tucked it away, giving his head a shake.

You are a clumsy fool. Is it no wonder the girl rejected you? No one wants you. How unfortunate it is, that we are saddled with the likes of you. You will never amount to anything. The countess's words breezed through his mind. He'd heard them so often these last two years that he almost believed them.

He would show her yet; very soon they would all receive their comeuppance in spades.

CHAPTER FIVE

Estelle woke from her faint feeling as if someone had hit her over the head with a hammer. Her eyes barely focused, but she instantly recognized she had been returned to her designated chamber. In a haze, she struggled to make sense of her surroundings. The fireplace glowed in doubles, confusing her even more. *What happened? Why do I feel this way?*

However confusing her current state left her, Estelle made out a shadow at the end of the bed, and it was not Ben. Whoever stood there observed her motionless, silent, and for some unknown reason, she did not sense a threatening presence. A gentleman came to her side and poured fluid onto a spoon.

"This will help with the headache."

He slipped the spoon between her parched lips.

Estelle tried to swallow, but could not help but choke at the bitterness of the medicine.

The man held a glass to her lips and poured some water gently into her mouth. "It has a disgusting taste, but I promise it will do you well. Go back to sleep, my love." *Why is this man calling me his love? I do not know who he is. Or do I?*

Estelle eased back into her pillow, waves of nausea rose from the pits of hell, and the smell of the smoke from the hearth began to irritate her. Yet, the sense that something was terribly wrong remained.

She shivered at a breeze passing over her inexplicably and the heat of someone's breath hovered by her ear.

"You must get away. Do not let him touch you. He will taint your soul, break your heart, and hell follows him everywhere he goes. Leave while you can."

Estelle tried to make sense of the words, but they were garbled. Her eyelids weighed heavily, her breathing became deep. She found herself being whisked away to a time before Ben proposed.

"Estelle, wait," Helen called out from down the street. "If you are going into Mr. Milton's perfumery, I would love to join you."

They walked in together and browsed along the proprietor's counter. The samples wafted up into the floral air, removing any trace of the city stench outside. Exotic scents of jasmine and cinnamon were Estelle's favorites.

Helen leaned in and whispered, "I just wanted you to know, I will be going away for a few months. I have an ailing relative in the country, but you cannot breathe a word of it to anyone. Not even my brother."

"Why would I tell your brother?"

"He is…how shall we say—He has formed an unnatural attachment to me, you see. He has also mentioned you in great detail, and has developed a—shh, here he comes."

She turned around and saw Edwin, who had to be nearly twenty-five now. It was not that he was not handsome or anything. His features were stark and patrician. There was something menacing in his demeanor in the way he walked, and the way he looked at her when he placed his hand on Helen's shoulder. Estelle curtseyed out of respect, but truth be told, she wanted to leave.

"Miss Humphrey; how delightful to see you again." Too soon for her liking.

"Have you been seducing my dear little sister with new perfumes?"

"Not at all. We were only browsing. Mr. Milton is known to have many delightful scents brought in from the Orient and the East Indies," she said.

He huffed and turned toward Helen. "I see. We need to go. Our uncle will not be pleased to find out we have been longer than we should have." Edwin turned away, dragging his sister behind him.

Helen looked back at her and brought a gloved finger to her lips, begging for silence.

"Helen, Edwin, please! Allow me to walk you back to your carriage," she pleaded, but they kept on walking out of the mercantile and onto the street.

Helen's request for secrecy was puzzling. She did not understand where in the world it was coming from considering two years passed since their uncle had been charged with their welfare, after their parents' untimely death in Scotland during a house fire. Edwin had been the sole survivor of the fire, while Helen had been away at school. She had not heard of any ill news from the Earl of Hawthorne's estate. In fact, if her memory served her right, Lady Cuthbert could not have been more pleased to have more children to dote on while her son attended school abroad.

They finally slowed down allowing Estelle to catch up, but the moment she linked her arm to Helen's, Edwin pulled her away. He tucked her hand into the crook of his arm, and leaned forward. The foul odor from his breath made her wince. How could one not be offended by such an unhygienic situation?

"I know we have not known each other long, Miss Humphrey, but I do wish to call on you some time. I plan on seeking your papa's permission to court you, if you would find that agreeable."

Her stomach turned at the asinine assumption. Helen said something about a carriage moving in their direction. She knew not if Helen was trying to distract her brother, or if she was trying to ask her something. It was not until she tripped and fell forward did she finally feel safe out of his reach.

Estelle recovered from her fall, but by then she was covered in mud. A merchant taking pity on her condition aided her. Edwin tried to assist, but the man told him to take his leave. She got up on her own, but quickly noticed how Helen was leaning away from everyone and shielding her middle.

What in the…

She could not be. Or could she? Helen had never mentioned being with anyone. Heaven pre-

vail! That explained her trip to the country. There had to be another way.

* * * *

Benedict rounded down the hallway, insisting on visiting her. The woman fainted dead away, and while he had carried her to her room, he had been quickly ushered out to allow the maids to undress her and see to her comforts. He worried for her constitution; it was not every day a woman witnessed a suicide. Or was it?

The Met would be swarming the estate within the hour. All the guests were warned not to leave as they'd all be questioned.

Not once in all his thirty years did he expect Gabriel to kill himself. As honest as they came, he never pegged Gabriel the cowardly type. He had even lent a hand with the hired help and his father's tenants. An all-round genuine fellow, and no matter how one might think they knew a person, it was hard to say what would drive a man to take his own life.

The halls were dark and sparsely lit. Shadows on the parquet flooring moved slowly, as if hellish apparitions rose from the floorboards. He approached a senior footman assigned to Estelle's door, giving him a quizzical look over, taking note of his features so that he would remember whom he spoke with. "Is there any news?"

The stark footman shook his head. "No, sir. Although, now that you mention it, I do recall hearing some noise a quarter hour ago. She might have briefly woken up for a drink of water."

"What do you mean she might have? Did you not go in and look on her?"

"No, sir. It wouldn't be proper. Besides, I was under the impression a maid would have stayed with her."

Benedict groaned, shoved the footman aside, and opened her door. The room appeared normal but upon further inspection, something did not feel right. He briefly glanced at Estelle to notice she slept soundly. He walked toward the fireplace and stoked the embers. Once satisfied the fire would continue to keep the room warm for a few more hours, he went to her bedside.

Benedict then noticed a single red rose, tied with a black ribbon at the end of the bed. What in the world? He picked up the rose, but it was the wrong time of the year for roses, and when he'd seen the gardens earlier, everything had withered away to shades of rust from the cool season that arrived early. *Where did this come from? Who's been here, and why would they leave this here?*

He took her hand into his after throwing the rose onto the nightstand. He brought her warm hand to his lips and pressed a kiss to her knuckles. How he looked forward to marrying her. From their first encounter, Estelle brought him much joy. In one month's time, he'd start a lifetime with her and show her every day how much he adored her.

Benedict squeezed her hand gently and her eyes opened wide with astonishment. He had startled her, and for that he was sorry.

"Ben, is that you?"

"Yes, it is, my love. How do you feel?"

She mumbled something and then brought her hand to cover her mouth as if she were going to be sick.

"Here, let me get you some water." When Benedict reached for the glass, he spied a spoon laden with some kind of liquid. He lifted the spoon, bringing it to his nose, and recoiled from the pungent but familiar scent.

"Dearest, did the maids give you laudanum earlier?"

"No," she replied with a glazed-over look.

Benedict felt the anger rising within him. If a maid had not been in here, then a man had been in her room, but it was not the footman. He would kill the man if he had stepped away from his post. He patted Estelle's leg and said that he would be back in a moment, leaving her bedside to question the servant. Benedict did not want to alarm her, as the effects of the medicine were still lingering, but he would get to the bottom of why someone would medicate her. Especially, after Gabriel had died in the house.

Did she see something she was not supposed to? He knew not of the answers, but he would be damned and figure them out himself.

"You there," he announced curtly. "Did you leave your post at all this evening since Miss Humphrey's arrival to her room?"

"No, sir. Well, I did, but I had a maid stand here in my stead until I returned from the convenience."

"I would like you to go and fetch a maid. I do not want Estelle alone inside her room.

I have errands to run, and I would like to speak with the earl."

"Certainly, sir. I will fetch the maid right away."

When the footman turned away and rushed down the corridor, Benedict returned to her bedside to find Estelle trying to get out of bed.

"Stay right where you are, dear. Tell me what you require and I will bring it to you."

"My shawl, Ben. The room is so drafty."

Was she mad? The room was stifling to the point he needed to begin removing layers. He loosened his necktie and removed his dinner jacket. After placing the two items on a chair by the door, he returned to her with the shawl.

"Estelle, the windows are closed and it is hotter than the pits of hell in here. If you are unwell, I would like to summon a physician to examine you."

"No!" she cried out, yanking the crocheted garment from his grip.

Benedict raised his hands in defeat. He had not meant to upset her so, but wanted to understand what ailed her. "I will not call for a physician, but I do not understand how you are saying it is drafty."

"Ben, I have something to tell you. It might sound odd."

"Go on."

"I saw her—Helen…earlier."

The maid walked in, dropping her tray with a gasp.

"Mary, are you all right?" Estelle asked with concern.

"Excuse me. I will clean up my mess, and bring another tray promptly."

"My dear, Helen has been gone for a year now. What you are saying is impossible."

She shook her head vehemently. "I swear it, Ben. Helen spoke to me, and she told me to stay away from him."

"Him? Who are you referring to, Estelle?"

She shrugged and pulled the covers over her legs.

This has to be the laudanum talking. Just what was it about this house that was making everyone mad?

The maid returned, this time managing to not drop the tray.

"No one, absolutely no one is to give her any medicine. Someone bloody gave her laudanum, and she is not talking straight. Look at her!"

"Yes, sir."

"Where is Lord Cuthbert? I have a need to discuss matters with him requiring immediate attention."

"In the library, sir; alone and quite angry at the moment. He discovered his favorite vase from the Orient destroyed beyond means of repair. He is in quite the fitting mood and likely to strangle someone. Consider yourself warned, my lord."

"Thank you," he nodded, "and I will be sure to remember that last fact before I say something that might infuriate him more."

Time to prod a bull and see what comes of it. There was a great mystery at work here and at this point the suspect could be anyone. He needed to discover more about the earl's dealings, and had to consider all the possibilities. What if there was a guest present who meant to destroy the earl, besides himself? They would of course stand in line, because if anyone would wrap the noose around Lord Cuthbert's neck, it would be him.

CHAPTER SIX

I t was mid-afternoon when Benedict reached the earl's library; a string of curses echoed into the hall. Before entering the room he carefully considered what he should mention to his host. He wanted answers just as much as the next person, but what ate away at him was who could have entered her room and administered the laudanum without even the footman or a maid noticing. One also couldn't ignore the fact that Gabriel's death wasn't mentioned again since that dreadful night. He'd heard some footmen later in the evening saying the body was moved to be collected by the authorities, but nothing more could be heard from where he stood in the shadows. The footmen must have known they weren't alone. A deception was at play, but who and why?

He considered how mad his future countess would appear if he mentioned her seeing visions of the earl's dead niece. In fact, they'd probably attempt to dissuade him to marry her as the only place she'd belong was in Bedlam. Nevertheless, it wasn't what she saw that bothered him as much as the warning she received. Estelle had been dead serious with what she saw. If Helen still haunted these halls, she had been wronged, but by whom? He'd experienced this once before, which was the only reason why Benedict gave merit to his fiancée's concern in the matter. He'd been very young, but recalled eavesdropping on his father's staff and secretly following them to the old abandoned stables several yards away from the new construction his father ordered. The dilapidated shack had been set fire to, with a stable hand trapped inside. Some say it was a jealous lovers spat, but all the staff were convinced the poor man haunted it ever since. With each passing minute, more questions emerged, and there wasn't an answer readily available.

Benedict quit hesitating and knocked on the door, waiting for an invitation. Moments later, a gust of air swooshed before him as the earl presented himself.

"What do you want? Do you know anything about my broken vase?" asked Lord Cuthbert.

He raised a brow at his host's stern and volatile tone. "I do not. I was too busy trying to figure out who has been in Estelle's room poisoning her with laudanum."

The earl took a step back, his eyes narrowed. He pursed his lips and inhaled sharply. "What do you mean she's been given laudanum?"

"I meant every word of what I said. If you will let me in, I have my own questions to ask you." He followed the earl in and waited to speak until he locked the library door. Benedict winced at the sight of the shards of glass strewn across the floor; then returned his gaze to his host who eyed him warily.

"How do you know that it was laudanum? Is it not possible your fiancée could have a problem that you are unaware of?"

Benedict scowled, his chest tightened, and the need to pummel the man for the insult rose to the surface. Never in his life had he heard such a ridiculous thought. Estelle never medicated herself, nor suffered any ailments to his immediate knowledge. The only time he'd ever seen a woman—his mother—seeking some sort of remedy, it was during her menses to ease her discomfort. A sorry truth he wished he didn't know about.

"I shall have you know, my lord, that Estelle addicted to pain medicine is about as likely as pigs flying. Someone gave it to her and I want to know who in this house would be in possession of such a drug."

The earl sat back in his seat and crossed his arms. Awareness flashed in his eyes, and it was in that time Benedict recognized the earl knew precisely who had access to such a powerful sedative in the house.

"I implore you, Lord Cuthbert. I must know who did this to her."

"I can assure you, St. John, the only person who would have access to laudanum wasn't the one who did it. Someone must have stolen it."

"What are you talking about? And how can you be certain of this?"

"Because it simply could not have been my wife. You know that as well. She was with me the entire time up until I came into my library to discover my vase destroyed."

The earl's admission still left the questions of who had stolen the drug and why feed it to Estelle. Again the thought caused him further worry. Had she seen something she shouldn't have?

"If that is the case, then who do you suppose would have had the opportunity to take the countess's medication?"

The earl exhaled and leaned forward, resting his arms on his desk. "I don't know, St. John, but I will find out. Now, if you don't mind, I'd like to have some peace."

Benedict inclined his head, left his seat, and returned to his room. He'd discover who the culprit was, and the earl wouldn't be able to save them.

* * * *

Estelle watched the maid move to and fro, cleaning and reorganizing, humming a somber tune she recognized from childhood. Every so often she caught the maid watching her, and then she'd get back to keeping busy, until the maid ended up sitting at her bedside.

"Miss Humphrey, I know we do not know each other, but—" She quivered and then continued, "But do you believe in spirits coming back on unfinished business?"

"I am starting to."

"If you do not mind my saying so, I heard you telling Lord St. John that you saw the master's niece. I should warn you this house is cursed. The servants are afraid of the master's nephew, Edwin, as well. Apparently every time he is around, someone gets hurt."

She never dreamed that Edwin held that much power over anyone; yet even Helen, before she mysteriously died, found her brother peculiar. What an odd inclination too. This house had way too many secrets and before she and Benedict left, she'd uncover some of its clandestine truths.

"Mary, did Helen have any journals or letters that the countess might have kept? If so, may I see them?"

"I do believe the countess had all of Helen's belongings brought to the attic in the west wing."

"Do you think you could take me some time?"

"I would be happy to, Miss, but it would be proper if his lordship showed you around. I do believe he had planned on doing so at some point tomorrow afternoon. However, I do not think that part of the house is anything he had in mind. From what I understood of the butler, a tour of the family's gallery and grounds is being arranged."

"But I do not wish to wait that long. Dash it." Estelle scowled, folding her arms across her chest, pondering how she could learn more about their surroundings and the family's history. Even more, the possibility of how much treachery lurked about this house.

"Do not be put out, Miss. While I cannot take you on a tour to the service and storage wings of the estate, there is, however, this." The maid went over to the paneled wall next to the hearth, uncovering a bookshelf. She withdrew a journal and returned to the bed with it, placing the leather bound item on Estelle's lap. "Miss Cuthbert carried herself quite gracefully and I am surprised she did not have men lined up in the courtyard. The silly chit spoke of aspirations beyond the traditional expectations of marriage. The gentleman who fell onto the terrace tonight...they were secretly engaged for a few months."

Helen never mentioned a secret betrothal. Estelle wondered why she kept it secret all that time and for how long? Unquestionably, her uncle knew something. One could not be so ignorant to the blissful state she would have been in, to be in love with someone.

Estelle opened the diary and skimmed through the pages, when a few letters fell out of the back. There were three letters addressed to Helen from Gabriel Templeton, her deceased fiancé and dead by the hands of whom? Had he been so distraught to take his own life at the same estate where his beloved perished?

The more Estelle pondered the subject, the more she desired to know just who exactly trespassed her room, and how they managed to escape without being caught by the footman outside of the chamber.

"Mary, I desperately want a tour of the home. Can you not simply just let me have a peek?"

The maid's eyes narrowed, and she turned away. "I am sorry, Miss Humphrey. I cannot and will not jeopardize my employment this night. However, if you find that you miss out on the excursion that his lordship has planned for tomorrow, I will then arrange for a quick tour. Until then, I would advise that you steer clear of the halls at night. There is no telling what kinds of specters haunt them, and with so many guests about, I do not want you to find yourself in any kind of conundrum. Besides, you are still recovering from the incident earlier today and I recommend that you rest. If you would like, I can summon your aunt?"

"Please, do not trouble her. She is up in her years and does require her rest. I will stay here, but if it is not too much trouble, I would like to know more about the family."

Mary placed her rag down and dragged a chair from the corner to her bedside. She folded her hands in her lap, licked her lips, and quietly whispered, "Where do you want me to begin?"

"From the beginning, or what you know of it."

"Hmm, I can only go back to what I have been told. The Marquess of Haverford, the earl's late father, inherited this estate shortly after the chapel burnt to a crisp. That is all I know, Lady Humphrey."

"How about just a short and quick tour of where Helen's things are kept, and I will never speak again on the subject?"

"Lord St. John might not be too pleased if you leave your room, but I suppose he won't be too angry if you are not alone. Let me see if I can arrange for one of the footmen to escort us."

The eager maid stuck her head out and whispered to the man guarding the door. He replied with a harshness to his voice, but Estelle could only make out his vow to source another footman to mind his post while he took them.

A knock on the door strayed her from her idle reflection. The bold footman popped his head into the room. "We best be going now, before someone gets suspicious."

Estelle jumped out of bed, no longer feeling the effects of the drugged haze, and wrapped her shawl around her tightly. They made their way through the house. Murmurs of conversations floated from within the rooms off the passages. Tension coiled up in her muscles, and yet excitement threatened to burst from her veins over their exploration. They reached another door when the footman turned to face her.

"Miss Humphrey, from this point on, we'll be using the service stairs to access the attic. Mind your Ps and Qs, and no one will think to question why you are travelling this way."

Estelle followed the footman with the maid continuing on from behind her. The dimly-lit corridor, combined with the sounds of servants climbing into their creaking beds, besieged her with an unsettling feeling of the calm before the storm. Since their arrival to Hawthorne Hall, this had been the first time she noticed the floorboards squeaking. Their instability mixed with the noisy sound of their footsteps sent shivers up her spine. It was not as if she weighed terribly heavy either. In truth, she weighed maybe a slight over seven stones. *This part of the house must have been a part of the old estate before it was rebuilt,* she speculated.

Estelle tugged on her maid's sleeve, leaned over and whispered, "Just how many service halls are there, Mary?"

"One for each wing, Miss. While we're permitted to use the main hallways, our mistress would prefer that we use those passages when transporting laundry or cleaning."

"One would think that's an awful lot of unused space for mischief."

"Indeed, Miss. Although most of the mischief lately has been committed in the openness of the manor."

"You'll have to show me which window Mr. Templeton fell from. I heard Ben telling one of his friends that he was not even in his room when the accident occurred."

The maid gasped loud enough for the footman to hear and he whispered back tersely, "Quiet, you two. We have another hall to follow and one last flight of stairs."

Their procession continued at the bottom of the next staircase. The footman reached for a candlestick and then began the ascent to a part of the house where, from the exterior, one would note a slight tower.

Two steps into her climb, Estelle heard a faint grunt and the sound of something being slid or scratched against a wall.

"Did you hear that, Mary?" she asked the maid.

Mary shrugged. "Hear what, Miss?"

"Someone is scratching the wall, but from the other side. How odd."

"I told you earlier, Miss. The house is haunted."

Estelle's heart hammered in her chest and her shoulders tensed. Too preoccupied by the notion of the manor being haunted, she ran into the back of the footman, who turned around and glared at the maid. "For the hundredth time, Mary, quit this haunted nonsense, or I will be telling the house-keeper about this unscheduled trip. I might also feel inclined to include, Miss Humphrey, that proper decorum would dictate one should ask their host for a tour of the premises during the day."

The footman scowled, and she knew it was her fault after all, but there was too much to be ex-plained, and at the rate things were going, no one was going to keep her informed. Besides, staying in her room would have been dreadfully dull and after her swoon, she did not care be in there alone.

The footman reached into his coat and pulled out a key. He pushed the door open, and the musty smell was so strong, she was forced to turn away, and missed that first glance into the empty room.

Estelle swatted the air, clearing the cloud of dust around her, and stepped into the attic. Dark places like these made adventure stories all the more surreal. What kind of secrets would she find in here? Would she uncover a murderous plot? Knowing that she wouldn't have too much time to explore, she walked around the small room, looking for a trunk or anything that appeared feminine.

"Over there, Miss, by the window. That is where the mistress wanted Helen's belongings moved to."

Estelle quickly made her way and opened the trunk. The top had been cluttered with articles of clothing and personal effects. Shifting the items to the side, she found some books and a bag. When she opened the bag, its contents felt like folded up pieces of paper, but the lack of light hindered any possibility to verify what they were. She pulled them out, and a book to hide them in. Estelle got up and closed the trunk, returning to the door where the maid and footman waited for her.

"What are you doing with that book, Miss?"

"I thought I should like to read it."

"The master has a well-stocked library. Why not choose something from there?"

"If Helen had a book stowed away, it is likely deemed more suitable for the female populace. I am sure nothing in your master's library is romantic."

The footman snorted and showed her the way out, ensuring he locked the door behind him.

"Come along now, you two. I think we have tarried long enough."

And that we have, I cannot wait to see what's in those letters. Estelle tugged on the maid's arm to pull her closer. "Do you think there is any chance my room can be changed?"

"I'm certain, but I will ask the housekeeper in the morning if it's possible."

Estelle couldn't possibly wait that long to see Ben. She'd have to wait until the maid left her, and would sneak into his room before anyone noticed.

How she hoped Ben would allow her to stay and keep him company. She wanted to be held, consoled, and she wanted to hear his sweet, deep voice until it lulled her to sleep. No longer was she satisfied with his soft fingers cradling her face while he kissed her gently; Estelle needed him in an unfamiliar, yet warm way.

These sentiments flooded her with a foreign desire. They had shared light intimate moments when her father left the room; Ben stepped closer to her one day, as she looked out of the window in the morning room, his arousal pressing against her bottom when he wrapped his arms around her, whispering of the delights in which they would both indulge. Behaving with decorum ceased to exist when he stood so close to her. Ben shared with her a deep connection she did not realize had ever existed before now. Why on earth did she feel so confused by these complex emotions?

Estelle supposed people married for less, but to truly be married to a person who loved and idolized her... If only her mama was here to see how content he made her.

CHAPTER SEVEN

Edwin paced the length of the passageway. Frantic and concerned that if someone were to closely examine where the gentleman had fallen from, his secret would be exposed. Seeing Estelle with her fiancé earlier did nothing for the anxiety and loneliness rising beneath his surface. How he longed to feel the soft touch of a woman, Estelle's in particular. No one understood that since Helen died.

His uncle and the countess were useless, too stuck on society and its niceties. They were too self-absorbed to even comprehend the menace living behind these walls. Sure, his past did not help, and if Edwin had an opportunity to turn back time, perhaps things would have been different. Yet, time could not be undone, and he would suffer eternally as would the rest of his bloody family.

"Quit your muttering, you fool. Someone is bound to hear us," his cousin growled quietly.

"Why are you even here, George? Should you not be chasing one of the married women or maids into a broom closet? Or has your cock suddenly disappeared?"

His cousin snorted. "Well now, at least you know what a cock is, but the question remains. Do you know how to use yours? I bet you are still a virgin." George began to pace as well and muttered, "You do realize that nosy bitch is going to expose everything. Something has to be done. If you had not gone to Gabriel Templeton's room, there would have been no issue. But no, you just had to interfere in matters that no longer concerned you."

"Helen was with child, you ignorant fool, of course something had to be done." "And what makes you think he fathered the child?" his cousin asked wryly.

"Why else would she have been engaged to him? I overheard her tell Mary one morning before she came down for breakfast."

"You and your spying. One of these days you are going to witness something that will throw you over the edge, and how I look forward to seeing your usual frantic and uncontrolled self, slip from all reality. Even better, that time will likely occur in front of the others, and much to your chagrin, it will be too late. Father will cart you away and have you locked up at Bedlam. Come to think of it, I fancy that thought."

Bedlam. Is that where they were thinking of putting me? The words stung; however, anywhere had to be better than living this lie.

"Is there any reason why you are here with me?" Edwin asked.

"As a matter of fact, there is. There's damning evidence in that attic, and that wench is manipulating her way to discovering what should never be found out."

Edwin pondered for a moment. What in the world could his cousin be hiding now?

"If you are so concerned that you are going to be found out, why don't you question Evan? If he has permitted something devious to occur and didn't report back to the earl, then mention it to the countess. I am sure your mother would do anything to protect her idiot son."

His cousin punched him in the gut, but before he slipped out into the hall, George cautioned him. "Make no mistake, cousin. If I am an idiot, then you are the simpleton. Do not underestimate my influence in this home."

The panel closed and Edwin once again stood in the shadows. Alone.

He winced at the pain. His constitution was deteriorating by the day, and he knew not of what ailed him. Edwin did his best to hide the lesions appearing on his chest, and discoloration on his arms he noticed some days ago. Part of him racked his brain as to why he was suddenly plagued with markings. What had he done to deserve such punishment? Yes, he'd done some horrible things, for which he'd answer for in his afterlife. But what brought on this illness?

Edwin gasped, cupping himself, remembering the tavern wench he caught up with weeks ago. *It had to have been her. What else could it possibly be?*

None of it really mattered at this point. By the time he was done ruining the remainder of his family, they would likely shoot him anyway. All he had to do was wait a few more days for correspondence from the Met in the village.

* * * *

Benedict had paced his room with worry and anger until his head could bear no more. He lay in bed and the loneliness swallowed him whole. In one month, he would share his bed with the love of his life and he'd never let her go. The frustration of wanting her so badly left him near on the edge of madness.

Hard with need, the only way he could seek relief had to be by his own volition. Benedict held himself and closed his eyes, imagining her taking him into her mouth, but the second he began to feel lost, he flung his eyes open at the sound of his door being opened and then closed.

Damn it! Did I not lock it?

Even more, Benedict could not hide his shock to see his fiancée standing there. "You should not be here, Estelle."

Oh, yes, you should, his body contradicted, betraying his own moral code.

"I do not want to be in my room. I want to spend the night with you."

"And what will your aunt do when she discovers you spent the night here?"

She grinned. "With any luck, she will disclose the scandalous behavior to my papa, and the wedding will be moved up." *Clever girl.*

He sat up and raised a brow. The girl had the worst timing. He was stiff—no— throbbing. He'd need divine intervention to not take her innocence tonight. Benedict waved her over and then patted the bed.

As she slid up next to him her eyes widened with surprise. "Ben, you are not wearing anything underneath your bed linens, are you?"

Benedict shook his head and found the blush sweeping across her face immensely pleasing. Evidently, his betrothed's virginity embarrassed her, even though he could not have been more relieved. He looked forward to corrupting her and turning her into a pleasure fiend.

"Does it bother you that I'm not?"

She nodded again, her blush now spreading to her neck. "But I..."

"I suppose, in order for you to get over your shyness, there would be no harm if you wanted to see my shaft."

She shook her head vehemently. "Oh, no. I could not...we cannot."

Benedict chuckled and pulled the sheets away and laughed as she slapped one hand over her mouth and the other over her eyes. The bed shook from his laughter. He could not contain himself any longer.

"Do not be afraid," he murmured as he placed a gentle kiss on the back of each of her hands before removing them. "While I had intended to wait until we were married, I shall like to show you how you can pleasure me, and I you, and still leave your hymen intact. That is, unless, you are eager to discover such pleasures beforehand?"

Benedict placed one of her hands on his chest and the other over his member. Her warm hand blissfully teased him. How he looked forward to sinking himself between those thighs and thrusting into her sweet, tight hole. "That's not so bad, is it?"

She shook her head and smiled. Her breathing had even relaxed. For tonight he'd spare her any further embarrassment and wait until she fell asleep before he took care of himself. Right now though, he'd pleasure her until he'd exhausted her. He wanted her head reeling from his ministrations, and ready to move to the next level of pleasure.

"Sweetheart, I would like you to remove your gown. But if you'd prefer, you may leave it on, but know that I will lift up your gown."

She gasped at the suggestion, but slowly complied with his request. Estelle was not very large. In fact, her petite stature made her appear as delicate as a glass doll from the Orient. Benedict straddled her. He reveled under her touch as she brushed her fingers over his nipples and the patch of hair trailing down his chest toward his shaft.

"Have you ever touched yourself, Estelle? Like here." Benedict caressed her breasts and then squeezed them. "Have you ever wondered what it would feel like to have someone touch, lick, bite, or pinch?"

He silenced her with a deep, passionate kiss, intent on dulling her mind with need. As his tongue rolled with hers, Benedict pinched the rosy bud of nipple and she groaned into his mouth. Lord, loving her would be the death of him.

Benedict pulled away and slid down her lithe body until his mouth reached her breast. This time he licked and suckled her breast as a man would, and then nipped at her nipple. Her bottom was raised sufficiently that his cock came close to make entrance, and he could not let that happen unless she permitted him.

He forced himself off and slid even further down, prying her thighs apart. Tonight promised to be a long night, but how he looked forward to delighting her.

Benedict continued with his ministrations, bringing his lips to the crest of her moist curls. The scent of her arousal drove him mad, to the point he desired nothing more than to ruin her, but he could not. Their time alone this evening, and her willingness to go this far, was a gift far greater than anything else. Besides, in no time they would be married and he would demonstrate his superior skills of lovemaking then. Now was the time to give her a sampling much like French chocolate drizzled over a sweet summer strawberry, served with the finest champagne to be had. His beloved deserved nothing but the best and he was going to give it to her.

He pressed his lips to her sex, suckling, and then moved downward and began lapping at her juices. Benedict smiled at the sensation of his fiancée cradling his head as he licked to his heart's content. Her moans of pleasure echoed around him, his own need bursting at the seams.

Benedict continued building up the pressure by dipping a finger into her dampness with a rhythm to match his licking. He picked up the speed without considering she'd release so soon. Her hands fell to his shoulders and her moans soon turned to whimpers.

Benedict braced himself for her undoing. As she released, he suckled harder and fingered her wetness with greater expediency until her body went limp and her legs collapsed at his sides. He moved up her body, hovering, and placed a gentle kiss on her lips and whispered, "And that, my dear, is what you have to look forward to."

Benedict rose to his knees to take care of his own need, which evidently would not take much time. He palmed his sac and then took his shaft, pumping it hard and fast. His fiancée lay there, watching him with a smile so large that one would think she wasn't an innocent.

Pressure rose in his belly and his sac tightened. His release imminent, he lowered himself to be closer to Estelle. Benedict lay down next to her and faced her to watch her expression change when his release came in a fury.

Hot, thick spurts coated her and her eyes widened with shock and embarrassment. Benedict couldn't help but smile. He placed his hand on the soft roundness of her middle, coating his finger with his seed. Benedict then placed his finger at the edge of her lips and purred, "Open up those delightful and sinful lips, my sweet. I want you to taste me."

She gasped, but complied with his request. Estelle swallowed hard and moved her lips, yet spoke no words.

"I see I've thoroughly shocked you. Take care, darling; next time, when we are married that is, I will show you how to take my shaft into your mouth, and give me pleasure the same way I did to you earlier tonight."

Her eyes widened again and she propped herself up. "Is that sort of thing what people really do? I was always under the impression that there was only two ways a man wanted a woman."

Benedict chuckled heartily and shook his head. "No, my dear. There are many ways to give pleasure. Tonight was only a tease of what our time together will be like." He turned to locate the washbasin and returned his attention to Estelle. "I will recover some linen and get you cleaned up. You need your rest and I need to find a clever way of returning you to your room before anyone notice you're not in there."

* * * *

Edwin groaned at the sight he happened upon. She should have been his, but no; fate had decided that Estelle should be with that man. The vision of the two of them in their scandalous tryst did appeal to him, and he could not help but run his hand against the rising bulge in his trousers. But soon the thought of the lesions, and possibly having contracted the French disease, made him gag.

Over the years, he wandered through these passages and spied upon their guests and inhabitants. He caught everyone, including the earl and his countess conducting affairs with other guests.

Ruinous ones at that; men with men, women cavorting with more than one man, couples betraying their solemn vows, and every one of them were of aristocratic blood. Yet, not one single event aroused him much like this one. Unlike his cousin's impression that he did not know how to use his own member, he could not have been more wrong.

The only difference between them was that his past liaisons were with willing servants and tavern wenches under agreeable circumstances, and he bore no prejudice to their gender.

A hissing noise behind caught him unexpectedly. He spun around to find George with a menacing grin.

"I see for once, you are actually observing some of the finer pleasures of fucking. What I would do in between those thighs for a night..." George's words trailed off into a whisper. "Of course, she would be bound and gagged, and I would probably sodomize her and kill her once I was done. You know, they're quite agreeable when they no longer breathe. They do not whine or gasp when you stuff their mouth with your cock, and they cannot scowl disapprovingly when you mention what else you want to do."

Rage blinded Edwin as he pushed his cousin away. "You will not touch her, do you understand?"

"And what do you suppose you will do? For all you know, I could slip in his room in the middle of the night, slit his throat, and do the very things I said a moment ago to that beautiful, stupid girl. I suppose if you wanted to watch, you—"

He lunged at George, only to miss his target. Pushed out of the way, Edwin hit the stone wall, knocking him senseless and dizzy. Before he could get up, his cousin straddled him and wrung his hands around his neck. Edwin gasped for air while trying to pull at his fingers, but in little time, his strength vanished, and darkness found him, taking him to a time and place he cared not to be.

"He has to go! I do not want that disgusting little imp in my house. Everyone knows he set the cottage on fire. Why must he stay with us?" the countess roared with contempt.

"Think of it as an opportunity to earn a little income, and when the time comes, we'll deem him unfit to live in society. I have some connections who would be easy enough to convince for the diagnosis. Have some faith in me, my lady."

Her scowl grew deeper and her brows furrowed with severity. "And what of his sister?

She's back any day now from that distasteful school. What shall we do with her?"

"Marry her off to the first sorry sod we can find. Although I've heard some rumors about some fellow in town having expressed an interest in her. Once I have the perfect chap in mind, we'll make all the arrangements."

"Very well. Until then, keep that beast out of my sight. I cannot be seen with either of them. Neither will be accepted by me, nor the society we associate with. They're mongrels! I cannot believe your father permitted your brother to marry that creature."

His uncle raised a brow at the insult, unaware that Edwin hid behind a column, eavesdropping. "My brother never did have a lick of sense. It's just as well they're out of their misery. That's what happens when you marry a traitorous lot."

CHAPTER EIGHT

The dining hall had been silent all throughout breakfast, until Lady Cuthbert broke the silence with laughter. "Well now, in lieu of last night's disaster, I daresay the masque we have planned tonight shall continue. Do you not agree, my lord?" she turned to ask the earl, who barely paid her any mind.

Estelle blanched at the suggestion, and turned to look at her fiancé, who already scowled with discontent at the announcement.

The earl coughed to mask her whispers. "Lady Cuthbert, I am sure our guests would think it ill-mannered if we were to proceed."

"Nonsense," exclaimed an elderly lady, smiling over her tea and toast.

"I agree," George added. "I think the lot of us could use some entertainment. Besides, I would like to get to know everyone better, my lord."

Estelle winced from the pang in her heart. The awful feeling something dreadful was going to happen struck her again. Out of the corner of her eye, she noticed two footmen being lured away. After having enough of this talk about a ball, she turned to Benedict and gave his knee a squeeze. "A most excellent breakfast, my lord. If everyone will excuse me, I am still feeling very tired. I think I shall retire for a bit."

"Do you not wish to stay on a bit longer? I had planned on giving the ladies a tour of the manor shortly," Lady Cuthbert crooned while setting her teacup down.

Estelle paused, trying to ponder how to get out of this invitation. "Perhaps another time, my lady. If you would do me the honor of showing me the grounds before I leave, I would be ever so gracious. However, I think it might be best that I lie down."

"Very well, my dear."

"Allow me to escort you to your room, Miss Humphrey?" Edwin asked, rising from his chair, looking back at his cousin and glaring at him.

"I think not, Edwin. I have yet to be formally introduced to Lord St. John's fiancée." George then turned to her. "It would be my pleasure to escort you," he growled quietly with a sinister smile.

Everyone stared at her, as if she had mysteriously grown a second head. She hardly understood the sudden interest in her. "Your offers are very kind, my lords, but I think I shall be fine on my own."

"Are you sure, dearest? After that envious display at breakfast between George and Edwin, I am not sure if I should be leaving you alone," Benedict mumbled under his breath.

Estelle only smiled, nodded, and then curtseyed before retreating to the hall.

Footsteps behind her approached while she stopped for a second at the bottom of the winding staircase.

"Estelle, wait," Ben called after her. "I will walk you to your room."

Did he plan on staying with her for the remainder of the morning, missing out on the opportunity to tour the grounds? Last night had been delightful in more ways than one. She did not expect to enjoy the level of intimacy he demonstrated. The memory of last night, of the way he used his tongue on her delicate parts, made her damp and eager with anticipation of what they would do next. *I wonder if he would allow me to do the same to him?*

"There you are, my girl. I had to ask myself what the rush was for, but I can see why. Those impertinent pups—you'd think the earl's nephew would know how to comport himself after your previous encounter with him in town."

She nodded, slipping her arm into his as they ascended the stairs. He tapped her hand and stopped at the landing before the next flight of stairs to where their apartments were. Light beamed in from the stained glass window, creating a myriad of dancing reflections on the wall. Ben released her arm but turned her to face him, gripping her arms.

"I do not want you alone with George. There are rumors circulating about devious things he has done, and I do not want you compromised in any way. You are mine; always remember that fact. I love you dearly, Estelle, and I would hate to have to kill a man who dares to touch you."

She blinked furiously at the callous words. How harsh, but what did her beloved know that she did not about the heir of Hawthorne Hall?

"I am touched, my love, but I do not understand why you seem to think I would allow another man to touch me. I am yours now, and always. Will you let me go, Ben? You are hurting me."

The intensity in his eyes washed away. He pulled her into an embrace, running his hand up and down her back, offering her comfort. In that moment, as safe as he made her feel, the back of her neck burned with the sense they were being watched. Ben's hand slid further down her back until it rested upon her bottom.

Estelle coughed to mask her worry. "Dearest, we should continue this conversation in private," she whispered, then continued. "We are not alone."

Estelle pulled away, holding out her hand, waiting for him to accept. He took it and resumed in taking the lead. The silence until they reached her room had been deafening. Yet, the unspoken words between them raced through her.

Benedict locked the door behind them, and he approached so swiftly she nearly lost her balance. His lips crushed hers, and beneath the harshness of his touch, she melted into him. The man could take her now, and she would not mind one bit.

"Take me, now. Please," Estelle pleaded, but soon found herself lifted and placed at the edge of her bed.

He knelt before her, resting his head on her lap. "My love, while I would love nothing more, it is too risky. For as long as we are here, the only time we can meet with some discretion will have to be at night." He paused and she saw the tenderness in his eyes. "Come to me tonight, and I will make sure you are satisfied fully."

Ugh. Estelle fell back onto her bed and sighed with disdain. "Why can we not just rush off to Scotland, Ben, and once we return we'll stay in town at The Langham until we've found a home?"

"As tempting as that thought may be, I simply cannot. You, my darling countess, will have a proper wedding. Are you not pleased by the news of a traditional wedding? I thought that by elevating you, things would be easier. Besides, I have plans and I would like nothing more than to include your father."

He left her sitting on the bed and crossed the room to stare out of the window. Later, he turned to face her and smiled softly. "I am sorry if my decision upsets you. I will do my best to make it up to you tonight. In the meanwhile, I should meet up with the rest of the guests for the tour. Are you sure you do not want to accompany your aunt and me?" Annoyed beyond belief, she fell back once again on her bed and grumbled, "No. I do not want to attend. I will sit in my room and mope about while trying to figure just what it is about this place that has me in such a foul disposition."

"Have it your way, my dear. I will have your aunt join you as soon as we return. Shall I have your maid come up and see to your needs?"

Estelle nodded then reached for a pillow and covered her face. The sound of the door closing echoed around her. All she had to do was wait it out and as soon as the earl, countess, and the remaining guests left, she would find Mary and discover what else was put away in the attic. There just had to be more secrets up there, waiting to be found out. She couldn't help but want to be the one to unravel the mystery of Helen's death, and whatever made this house so cursed.

* * * *

Benedict hated leaving her behind. The disappointment that splashed across her face when he declined in taking her when she most desired him left him feeling cold and unhappy. Who was he to decline the woman he was planning on marrying anyway? Yet, his moral obligation to keep her free from any further scandalous situations settled in. His body urged him to do so, but he could not risk the possibility of them being caught. While he did not mind their reckless behavior, her Aunt Margaret would have an apoplectic fit. No, Estelle would have to wait until tonight.

"Please tell me, St. John. What are your plans in the near future other than marrying that delightful creature of yours? When you return from your honeymoon, I am ready and available to introduce you to the other lords of the clubs I attend. For I am certain they will be most eager for an introduction," the Earl of Hawthorne said candidly.

"You are too kind, my lord. I would certainly appreciate your assistance and to meet your comrades. I am sure more connections will come in handy. However, I have quite a bit of work to do before I begin gracing the clubs of London. In particular, I'm exploring the idea of having a new home built, but want to assess the existing real estate in town first."

"Very well, young man. I look forward to calling on you and your countess when the papers have been finalized."

The earl gazed upon the guests who walked lazily through the terrace and down the path toward the old chapel that burnt to the ground fifty years prior. Benedict found himself instantly drawn to the recollections the man was evidently remembering. He followed the earl's eyes to the chapel and wondered if the man had a good upbringing. Benedict surmised it would have been a proper one, but by London standards proper did not always equate to a loving parentage.

"My lord, as you already know, the manor's history is speculated much. Would you mind sharing what you know of your ancestors and the land on which the manor is upon? Plainly, there is much history here," Benedict said.

"There is much to be told about Hawthorne Hall. Although, I am not certain now is the time..."

A howling beyond the cook's garden alerted them all. The remaining guests stilled on the path.

Benedict raced over to his beloved's aunt paling at the horrific sound. "Benedict, do tell me that sound is not being made by a wolf."

The earl came to a halt and turned to face Aunt Margaret. "My lady, wolves have been extinct in these parts for centuries. I imagine it would be some sort of animal that is trapped. Do not worry. I will have someone investigate. Let us carry on to the chapel and I will share the history of the building. Come along, everyone," the earl coaxed, trying to cover up wherever the sound hailed from.

A gleam in the earl's eye exuded an awareness and certainty, and if he were a betting man, the earl most definitely had an idea of what was transpiring. Either that or he clearly had a guilty conscience.

Benedict took Aunt Margaret's arm and hooked it in with his, and was about to follow the group when a shadow moved swiftly from the corner of his eye. *What in damnation?* He turned his attention toward the garden and caught a door closing behind some ferns. From this distance, which had to have been at least twenty yards away, the entry was not at all noticeable. *What lay behind that door? Could the noise that frightened the guests be coming from there?* He had so many questions and not enough time to explore them.

He and his companion followed the others, and while Estelle's aunt paid thorough attention to the earl's tale, Benedict could not help but think if the area in question connected to the part they slept in. Completely ignoring what the group had been discussing, he bent down to whisper to Estelle's aunt. "I know this might sound odd, but Estelle has been behaving quite peculiar since the tragedy. Perhaps you could speak with her. I am certain she will be more forthcoming with you."

Her aunt nodded. "I will check on her the instant we return to the manor. Although, I think it best that we pay attention to our gracious host.

He has looked our way several times, scowling. I do not think the earl likes being ignored."

"An aristocratic trait, my lady. Most men of the peerage are not satisfied until they are the center of attention. Let us resume our focus on him and once we return to the house, we will continue our discussion."

Benedict strode toward the group now leaving the family cemetery. There was much to be discovered and very soon he would have answers to save his father from being blackmailed further.

* * * *

Estelle groaned for what seemed the millionth time these last thirty minutes. "That is it. I'm going on my own and if Mary will not show me, I will find someone who will."

She bolted from her room in search of a servant who could lead her to her maid, but luckily she did not have to engage anyone else in her foibles.

Mary stood whispering to another servant at the end of the hall.

"Mary, I apologize for interrupting but—" Her words were cut off by a distant howl. The hairs on the back of her neck stood on end, and a shiver licked up her spine. "What in the world made that sound?"

The servant Mary had been speaking with hastily ran away, leaving the two of them together to discuss in privacy. "I haven't the slightest clue, Miss. However, I can assure you most of the staff is suspicious. I hardly imagine the sound being made by any animal. Which leaves the question of who is making that noise and why?" Her maid stopped and scowled. "I had been informed by your fiancé that you stayed behind, that you were not feeling well. Should I assume you stayed behind on purpose?"

Estelle pursed her lips and put her hands on her hips. "Would it really matter why I stayed behind? If you must know, I was cross with Ben and in ill-spirit after he declined a particular request. I am, however, looking to take you up on that offer of showing me around. There wouldn't be much sense in joining the others at this point, considering they're probably already on their way back from the tour."

"What tour did you promise, Mary?" a footman asked, his eyes narrowed and his lips pursed as he rounded the corner and approached them.

Suddenly ridden with guilt for having put the maid in an awkward position, Estelle went to speak up, but the man raised a hand to silence her.

How impertinent! Who does he think he is to silence me in such a way?

"Why are you promising things that you cannot deliver, Mary?"

"I only meant it as an alternative, Evan. Most of the guests will have already seen the estate except her. Since that unfortunate incident yesterday, I would think you of all people would be fine with a small tour. Why don't you accompany us?"

"I cannot, nor will I be a party to this misguided adventure. I never thought you would be so foolish," Evan said.

Estelle desperately wanted to intervene, but when she went to speak, both servants silenced her this time.

"Evan, I will show her around. The question is, will you not give her the tour? She is most anxious to see some of the older parts of the estate. Did you know she was friends with the master's niece?"

The footman rolled his eyes. "Fine, I will escort you, but right now is a bad time. Perhaps when things have settled down for the evening, I will show you around the parts that no one resides in, except for the servants, that is."

Estelle smiled then, knowing that her maid had kept her promise, albeit it involved coercing the footman, but, nonetheless, her manipulation worked.

After returning to her room, she flounced onto the bed, occasionally staring at the mirror that haunted her upon her arrival. There had to be a perfect explanation for all that transpired here, and she hardly suspected ghosts had anything to do with it. She couldn't help but ponder if Ben managed to get any further with his unofficial investigation. He should have discovered something by now, to keep his father safe and their family's reputation intact?

Nevertheless, they would be gone from this place, and no matter the size of the scandal, Ben would ensure they were all safe.

* * * *

Benedict stalked down the hall toward his room, mourning that it would be some time before Estelle would join him again. Last night had been an incredible display of his restraint. He did not know that he could remain so calm, even when she lay next to him. Estelle in his bed seemed natural; they fit perfectly in all senses. She balanced his stark moods, and his straight and narrow sensibilities.

Yet, when they were in the room together for more than ten minutes, he wanted to bed her, mark her as his, and never leave her side. *Lord, why did no one ever tell me that love could turn your thoughts to mush?*

About to open his door, a servant approached him from behind.

"Sir, my lady wishes to speak with you in the master's office. Come along now."

He wondered what this could even be about. He did not think he'd done anything wrong, nor Estelle.

Benedict entered the brightly lit room where intricately and ornate designed bookcases lined the walls. Lord Cuthbert sat behind his desk, and his scowling wife stood next to him.

"There you are, my good fellow. I hope we did not catch you at a most inopportune time?"

"Not at all, my lord. I was only resting before the masque tonight."

"Ah, yes." The earl turned to his wife and frowned, and then returned his focus to him. "The reason I called you here, is that it has been brought to my attention that your fiancée is in possession of an item that belongs to my dead niece. And most disturbingly, that it had been stolen from the attic late last night. Can you explain these offenses?"

What in damnation is he talking about? Estelle never mentioned about taking an unexpected tour to the attic, nor did she advise him of any items she might have removed from there.

"My lord, I assure you, I know nothing of the sort. While I have no explanation for Estelle's actions, I can say that she and Helen were friends before that unfortunate business. I will speak with her tonight, and if she did remove something, I will see that it is returned myself."

"Excellent, my good man." He turned to his wife, and waved for her to leave their presence.

The countess began, "But—"

"No buts, woman. I have business to discuss with Lord St. John. Now off with you."

The countess, clearly cross and unhappy with her dismissal, left the room, slamming the door behind her, leaving the glasses on the sideboard rattling as if the ground shook with fury.

"I apologize for the hastiness in this meeting, but you can understand why. I want you to know, that if Miss Humphrey wanted something, as a personal reminder of Helen, all she needed to do was ask. I would be more than happy to oblige any friend of my beloved late niece."

"I will be sure to inform her, my lord. What is it that you wished to speak with me about?"

"My son George. As you well know, he has returned from the continent and I need him to find some useful employment. Your father was considerate referring one of his men for the position, and the gent has done an impeccable job keeping on top of my tenants. It is my hope that your father and his man of affairs will help educate my son. I have no time to instruct him myself. Besides, I believe your father owes me a boon or two, and this task should settle it. I would like for George to take over those duties as soon as he is able to."

Lord, how could Cuthbert think of saddling George on his father and secretary? What more could the man be plotting? No man deserved to be treated thusly.

"Lord St. John, try not to be so put out. I will pay your father's secretary a handsome severance, and I will even ensure he gets my recommendation for ongoing employment elsewhere in addition to his service to your family. I have it on good authority that the Earl of Weston is in need of a man who is good with numbers, and discretion."

"I understand. Albeit it will be a hard thing to explain to my father's secretary that he is no longer needed. I know not of what he'll say to the offer and recommendation. For all we know, he will want to retire. My mother keeps reminding him that he should take his wife to the country, now that their boys have all married off. I will mention the recommendation to him and send word. In the meanwhile, does George know of your plans for him?"

The aging earl stared at him with a quizzical brow. "No. I have every intention of informing him tonight during the masque, and contacting your father within a fortnight as we had plans to meet."

Of course he'd deliver his decision in the presence of a full manor, all the more to keep the young man's temper in check. He did not know much of the earl's heir other than what he learned during their time in school, and what he had heard was not pleasant. He'd heard from his friends that George was frequently uneasy in his mind, most especially ones that involved women, his taste for young ones, and a rather wicked penchant for taking them against their will. Rumors they were, and unless he'd heard them himself, he'd pay them no mind. But everyone knew there was an ounce of truth to every tale.

He'd have to inquire with his friends some more. If the man oozed trouble, and he had just arrived from the continent, it would be only a matter of time before news drifted from his stays abroad. And if there was something he knew: news from an ill-mannered brat would travel like fire.

Benedict raised his brows and glanced over at the grey display out of the windows. "Was that all, my lord?"

"Actually, no. There is also one other matter I wish to discuss with you. I find that you are the only one I am able to confide in, but I do not know what else to do. With the understanding that my son will be managing my other estates, I feel obligated to ensure employment for my nephew. The boy is odd, and his unhealthy attachment to his sister became worse when she died. I often thought that he needed some time away, but after the fire out in the country at my sister's cottage, it was a miracle he even survived."

So the earl's nephew was troubled. What in the world did that have to do with him? Why not hire a physician? Even better, send him to a hospital. It wasn't uncommon for a mind to become troubled after a tragedy. Why not discuss these plans with the boy?

"My lord, where are you going with all this information?"

"I have heard the servants' whispers, saying the walls talk late at night. And I have also seen the fear in their eyes of late. Since the death of your friend Gabriel, nothing has been quite right. My boys have been skittish, silent, and awkward. I haven't the slightest clue what has the boys behaving so peculiar. I do know that things were quiet before Edwin joined us and I would like things to return the same way. Seeing as you will be returning to London soon, I would like you to make inquiries on my behest."

"What kind of inquiries are you talking about?"

"The kind that employs citizens who might be slightly disturbed and ill. He spends a great deal of time in the neighboring village, doing what, only the good Lord knows. I have heard that he's spent a good deal of time at the tavern. Although, I have no clue as to what he's doing. I can't foresee any wench tending to a man of his capacity."

"I do not mean to sound insensitive, my lord, but perhaps it is best he is examined first. If he is truly troubled, would you allow it on your conscience to release him in town, only for him to embarrass you, or your family?"

"Young man, I am not new to scandal. I have had my fair share. Speaking of which, have you heard what is being said about George? The countess had heard on an outing with other ladies that our son became mixed up with some French noble lady, a married one at that. Such vicious gossip."

"What if it were true Lord Cuthbert, what would you do? An affair with a married woman—what if she became pregnant?"

"I will not have any of it. Damn it all to hell. Just find my blasted nephew a job. Once this masquerade is over, and George has been informed of all these plans, I think it is best that Lady Cuthbert and I take up permanent residence in our home in Scotland."

"And what of this house? You won't leave George here with your nephew and full staff."

The elderly man scoffed and slapped the flat of his desk. "Of course not. George can move to my townhouse, and well, Edwin will have his own place too. I have been thinking of selling this place for some time now."

What a way to end his legacy. The old goat would not leave the estate to his son, which meant he did not even trust his son to manage the entirety of it. Did the man suspect what his son has been up to?

"I do believe that is all I wanted to discuss. I apologize for having taken up the majority of your afternoon. I am sure you'll want to be seeing that lovely fiancée of yours. She is certainly one you do not want out of sight for too long. A woman that beautiful ought to be shackled to her apartment."

Just what did the earl mean by that? Estelle was an intelligent woman, who came from a good family. She wasn't a broodmare, nor did he intend to keep her hidden away in their house once they were married.

Benedict reached the end of the corridor when he noticed the earl's nephew listening outside Estelle's door. Benedict stopped to watch, but when the fool remained at the door with his ear firmly planted, he had to stop the invasion of privacy.

"You there, Edwin! What do you think you are doing?"

The moment he approached Estelle's door, Edwin took off, nearly tripping himself on a runner at the end of the hall. Benedict sighed deeply. About to knock, the maid swung the door open.

"Master Edwin, what on earth has gotten into you?" The maid scowled and turned toward him.

"Oh, my. My apologies, Lord St. John. Miss Humphrey is just taking a little rest before the ball tonight. Can I get you anything?"

"No, Mary, that will be all. Continue with your duties, and if you find out why that rascal was at my fiancée's door, I must be told immediately." *I will wait until tonight to inform her of my findings.*

CHAPTER NINE

"Good God. This gown is too tight. Surely, Benedict will object how snug it fits around my waist and all," Estelle said.

"Such nonsense. The man adores you, and if anything, this gown will make him want to run to the altar posthaste."

Estelle sighed and continued to suck in her breath while the maid aided her in tightening her corset from behind. The elaborate gown had been a gift from Benedict, and the mask had been from his mother's supposedly extravagant collection.

"Miss, I had an idea about your hair. If we curled and then pinned it up, the mask would sit perfectly and undisturbed."

"Very well. I can't wait to see how you arrange my hair."

Mary tugged, separated, and worked wonders with Estelle's dark hair.

Estelle stared into the mirror, admiring the riotous curls framing the golden mask, ornately jeweled with red and blue faux gems. The colors blended nicely with the midnight blue French style gown made of silk. She could only imagine the small fortune Benedict had paid for the ensemble, and she couldn't guess when she would wear it next. "I think you are right, Mary, the hair looks utterly divine this way."

"We need to hurry though, as your handsome fiancé will be arriving any time now to escort you to the ballroom."

A faint snort somewhere in the room could be heard, making the hairs on the back of Estelle's neck stand on end.

"Are you all right, Miss?"

Estelle turned her head to face the maid. "I am, but did you hear that?"

"I thought that was you," the maid said, looking astonished and perplexed. "We're the only ones in here, Miss. I cannot imagine what the noise could be. I told you this house is cursed. I swear it, the ghosts of its past haunts the halls at night. Voices, furniture being dragged, it's all wrong."

Estelle reached to take the woman's hands into hers. "Now, now, do not let that imagination of yours go running. I am sure there's a perfect explanation for what is happening here."

The possibility that rodents cavorted behind the walls sent a shiver up her spine. The manor had been partially rebuilt, so what if the original estate had remaining passages, or holes in the cellar that rodents came in through the house? Anything at this point could be possible. *What I really want to do is explore on my own.*

A knock at the door startled the poor maid as Estelle watched the reflection bounce. "Come in," Estelle called out, returning her attention to her maid's expert hands.

"How stunning, my dear. Would it be improper of me to say you look ravishing tonight?"

Estelle giggled. Whenever Benedict put on such airs of pretension and nobility, they'd always managed to make fools of themselves in public. Waiting for her maid to step away, Ben had taken the mask from her hands and set it on her face.

"Now, up you go. I want to see the whole picture complete with a turn around the room."

Estelle rose from her seat and twirled for him. When she finally stopped, she even curtseyed to humor him.

"That's my girl. You look absolutely stunning, dearest."

"And you, my handsome rogue, look as mysterious as ever."

"We should be on our way, my dear. I am pretty certain everyone will come searching for us. The music has already started, and I am sure you are eager to mingle with the others."

"Yes, but this whole ball should have waited. It is not proper, Ben. There has been one death and odd behavior and sounds surrounding us at night. What kind of hosts are they to celebrate when there's much to worry about? Besides, I've heard whispers that an inspector is due to arrive anytime now."

"You don't say." Ben raised a brow and whispered, "You'll have to tell me more when we're alone next."

Deep down, Estelle knew their hosts concealed many secrets and the question remained; what were they? Not to mention, did she really want to be caught in the middle of anything more scandalous than what was already occurring with her future father-inlaw?

Later, they were joined in the hallway by her aunt. "I was beginning to wonder what you two were up to, and I can see why. You look positively elegant, Estelle. It's a pity your papa isn't joining us this week."

"Do you really think so? The style of the gown is comparable to the extravagant gowns Marie

Antoinette used to wear in court. Benedict spoils me so."

"He does, indeed, and if this is any indication of what your marriage will be like, you'd best be giving him all the attention he deserves, my dear," her aunt said.

Estelle watched her fiancé's smitten smile turn into a warm, comforting one as he took her aunt's hands into his. "Aunt Margaret, Estelle is one of the most wonderful women I know, next to you, of course. I would spoil her naturally, and all within reason. I can assure you, she'll be well cared for."

Estelle followed along, completely amused by the discussion her aunt and her beloved were having. Nothing gave her greater joy than to witness love between them. As they approached the ballroom, the noise spilled out of the hall. Guests danced and laughed and were making conversations with each other.

Their host now approached them merrily and bowed before Estelle. "My dear, may I have this dance with you?"

Estelle glanced over at her fiancé, who nodded with approval. Accepting the earl's hand, she followed him into the ballroom where the remaining guests danced. Ladies' skirts swished around her and the echoing sound of the music being played in the corner of the room overpowered the muffled discussion.

The ballroom had been a part of the old building. From the molding to the intricate carvings on the paneling, the ambience of the room amidst the soft lighting of candles strategically placed throughout embodied mystery and continental charm.

Estelle observed her fiancé leading her aunt to the dance floor. The two seemed amused at the opportunity to relax.

"Do not worry, my dear, your fiancé will not disappear. I do believe he is quite safe with your aunt," the earl mentioned before continuing mid-turn. "Tell me how you met

Lord St. John. It was my understanding that before the two of you were engaged, you had a bevy of suitors."

A bevy? What on earth had the man heard of me? "I am not certain what you mean, my lord. Yes, I have had suitors before, but none that had any honorable intentions, or my papa approved. But of course, you are probably meaning your nephew. I had met him a few times and he had written to me. I'd been clear from the beginning that I had no designs on him."

"Ah, so you do remember my nephew. Of course you do. What did you find so repulsive about him? Was it his unnatural affection for his sister? Did you know that she planned on leaving us to go to the country?"

Estelle found herself taken aback by the earl's questioning. His insistence worried her, and made her wonder how much the earl knew of the murder and Helen's unresolved death. Did he suspect why his niece planned on leaving their estate a year ago? Did he know more than what the investigators concluded? *The Examiner* had published that the Met didn't suspect foul play, and it was nothing more than a tragic accident. *Who tumbles out of window by accident…much in the same way Gabriel did?*

Someone tapped Estelle on her shoulder, cutting the earl out of his position on the dance floor, and she soon found herself dancing with his son George. Estelle inclined her head. "My lord."

"No need for the formality, sweetheart, the pleasure is all mine. It isn't every day I get to dance with a beautiful lady such as yourself."

Estelle felt her cheeks sear with embarrassment from the compliment. "I am sure you say that to all the ladies, but thank you."

Estelle followed the earl's heir's lead and danced until the music stopped. The music had barely halted when Benedict appeared at her side and wrapped his arm around her waist.

George glared at him with an icy gaze, sending shivers up her spine.

Ben leaned into her and whispered in her ear, "I need to talk to you about something, let us leave the ballroom."

Estelle nodded and curtseyed, but before she could pull away, her dance partner raised her hand to his lips and pressed a kiss to her gloved hand.

"It's been a pleasure, Miss Humphrey."

She didn't even have the opportunity to thank him when Benedict pulled her away. He did not even say why they needed to talk, but his rigid form was indicative of him being cross.

I wonder what happened.

* * * *

Benedict had not meant to tug her along, but he could not stand the earl's son. The way he'd seen the earl speaking to her during their dance made him curious to find out why Estelle looked horrified.

He found a door leading out to the terrace and walked into the moonlit garden until they found a secluded spot to sit. Benedict knelt before her and took her trembling hands into his, squeezing them to offer some comfort before their discussion. Yet, no matter how he proceeded, she would either hate him, or take her leave and return to her room. "Estelle, you know I would walk through the pits of hell for you, right?" She nodded, biting her lower lip.

"You have to promise to be honest with me, my dear. Why did you go to the attic the other night, and why did you take something that belonged to the earl's late niece?"

"Ben, you must not think ill of me. There is something not quite right here. Besides, I wanted to see if I could find out more about what happened. We need to leave as soon as we can, Ben. This place is haunted, eerie, and the servants are just—strange."

He understood Estelle's fear, but there had to be truths uncovered before they left. Ben could not leave like this. He needed whatever she took from the attic returned, and to find out why Gabriel Templeton was targeted or if it was a suicide. To take his own life after being invited to the home of the woman he wanted to marry? Certainly that was how the law would ascertain what occurred here. However, he suspected there was more to the story.

"Will you give me what you took from our host's attic, please? I will see that it is returned to Lord Cuthbert, and once I have settled and satisfied Scotland Yard's curiosity about Gabriel's death, we shall leave."

"Do you swear it?"

Benedict cupped her cheeks and pulled her closer toward him. "I would never lie to you, my dear. I only want to protect you. Besides, the faster we return to town, the sooner we'll be able to protect my father from the earl and be married. Come now, let us walk to your room and I will collect the item you borrowed."

"But what of my aunt? We left her behind in the ballroom."

"I am certain she will not object to my escorting you."

She smiled up at him and wrapped her arms around him. Lord, how he loved the way she smelled, and the more they stood this close together, the more he wanted to take her to his bed again.

Benedict crushed his lips to hers only to be interrupted by the sound of the door opening.

"There you are. I have been looking all over the place for you two," Aunt Margaret exclaimed, standing by the door with her arms crossed.

"We were just heading indoors. Estelle expressed an interest in retiring early, so I thought I would talk to her privately before escorting her to her chambers. Would you like to join us?"

"No. I think I will return to the festivities, my dear." She focused her quizzical gaze toward Estelle. "We will be joining the countess for breakfast with several other guests at eight o'clock sharp. Do be sure to tell your maid that you need to be ready and downstairs by a quarter to eight. We should always arrive before the actual scheduled time. It would be rude for us to keep her ladyship waiting."

"Yes, Aunt Margaret. I will be down in time in the morning. I shan't disappoint you."

Her aunt returned to the room where some lady friends were waiting eagerly to chat with her, while Benedict and Estelle continued on their way up to her room.

Benedict could not ignore the niggling feeling that they were being watched. Yet, the halls were silent, and only the occasional servant passed them. All the guests were downstairs being entertained, while they were alone. He squeezed her hand a little tighter when they reached her door. When he placed his hand on the knob, Mary pulled the door open, nearly colliding into them.

"Oh! I am begging your pardon, Miss. I came to see the room prepared before you retired for the evening. Is there anything I can get you before you go to bed?"

Estelle shook her head. "No, Mary. That would be fine."

The maid smiled and left them alone, which he found amusing. As inappropriate as escorting Estelle into her room was, he'd never intended to scandalize her, unless, she wanted it to go that far.

"I left it over here, Ben. Honestly, my intentions weren't to rob the earl. I just wanted to see what belongings remained of Helen. If it isn't too impertinent for me to say so, I have a feeling she knew of the troubles here. The last time I saw her, she behaved rather odd."

Benedict closed the door behind him, ensuring he locked it so that they were free from interruption. Halfway across the room as he passed her bed, he felt a cold draft. He looked up to see the windows were closed and the drapes had not moved from their stationary position.

How can it possibly be drafty in here? The fire had been stoked. Something was definitely not right.

"Ben, are you all right? You look vexed."

Benedict found himself in a daze. Something about this room did not sit well with him, and he could not quite put his finger on it just yet. His attention on the mystery of Estelle's room broke when she handed him a book. "What's this?"

"This is the book I took from the attic. It belonged to Helen. I am really sorry if this has caused you any undue stress and poor relations, Ben. Honestly, had I known this trip would end up this way, I would have declined your invitation to accompany you."

"Do not worry about a thing, dearest. Tell me though, how are you finding this room? There seems to be something off, and I cannot quite place my finger on it."

She gave him a bemused look. Would she think him crazy for asking such a question?

"Darling, why don't you come sit next to me on the bed and relax? You don't look well, and I would not mind curling up next to you. I have missed you terribly since our second night here. Would you mind spending the night with me?

That is, you'd have to leave before the servants got up."

"You do realize if we are caught, your aunt will probably have you on the next coach back to London."

"Mm-hmm, but I do not mind. We'll be married soon enough."

Benedict followed her to the bed, placed the book on the nightstand, and slid up next to her. While they were still clothed, the chill had not quite escaped the area. He reached for a blanket and covered their legs with it. Benedict pulled her into his arms and closed his eyes to rest.

He hadn't realized how tired he'd been until now, what with the exhaustion from mingling with the others and running back and forth on this large estate. And yet, no matter how much running around he did, when Estelle stood at his side, he forgot all his obligations. How he loved her so.

He felt her breathing slow down; she had fallen asleep in his arms all too easily. If this was what he had to look forward to, Ben knew he had found his mate for life. He'd stay the night with her, giving her comfort in a way that they both needed.

This house began to weigh on him heavily in a psychological manner.

Was it any wonder why Scotland Yard insisted on interrogating everyone?

Especially as it had been a year since the earl's niece had died. He had heard the whispers of a suicide pact, but no one knew for certain.

This house had far too many secrets, and he would discuss with his remaining friends what he knew of the family. Duncan's family knew the earl's very well; perhaps he could add some insight to their trouble, finances, and maybe their son's mischief abroad.

Benedict sighed and found himself drifting off. He knew not of how much time had passed since he'd closed his eyes the first time, but when he blinked them open briefly, the room had gone dark.

"Damn it!"

He heard an oath whispered, and a gust of wind behind him made him shiver. *Blast it! I will have to find that draft. I will not have Estelle catching her death.*

The room went silent again and Estelle remained asleep—her head neatly tucked beneath his chin—when he sensed they weren't alone. Darkness shrouded the movement around them, and for a glimmer of a moment, he felt the presence before him at the bedside. A few seconds later, footsteps moved and he heard a door sliding.

Benedict leapt at the opportunity to turn and see the paneled wall next to the bed close. *So that's why it has been so drafty in here. A secret passageway. But where does it lead to, and who the hell is coming in here? It is time to get to the bottom of this.*

He'd start immediately, by having Estelle moved out of this room and in with her aunt.

He had enough of all this intrigue. Whoever had given her the laudanum that first night had crept into this room via the hidden passage.

Benedict climbed out of bed and crossed the room to the hearth and lit a new fire. Satisfied with sufficient light, he grabbed a candlestick and placed it on a table near the passage entry. He scanned the wall for some kind of mechanism to trigger the release of the door. Nothing out of the ordinary stood out, but when he slid his palm over a raised etching, a *swoosh* at his feet and a *pop* above him alerted him that the panel opened.

He took the candle after opening the door, and lit the way before him, a dark and dank corridor masked in cobwebs, river-rock, and the remains of dead rodents. Lord, 'twas a sight that would frighten any sensible woman. What if the same person that crept into Estelle's room did the same to Helen? Did the earl know of this passageway, and where did it lead to?

"Ben, where are you? What in the—"

Benedict turned around to find his fiancée standing at the entrance to her room. Tears filled her eyes, and she clutched her chest. "Is…is this how someone got into my room?" she asked in a low, frightened whisper.

"If I had to guess, yes, although, now remains even more questions; who and why?" "Where does this lead to?"

"I have no idea, but I am not wanting to find out just yet. Come along now, we'll get you back to bed, and I will take this issue up with our host in the morning. As far as I am concerned, this room is not safe, and the culprit needs to be caught immediately." Ben led them out of the hall, and closed the door behind them.

I will find out who's behind this, even if it is the last thing I do.

After ushering Estelle into her room, he made his way down the hall to find a maid to stay with her, and then he headed into the games room to ponder over his own findings. He couldn't help but wonder why so many guests attended in honor of George.

If they had any lick of sense, they would steer clear of this family, yet was it possible they too were in a similar situation? His own invitation appeared suspicious and if his hypothesis was correct, he was lured here to keep him from interfering with his father's affairs. What the earl didn't suspect was that he already knew of the demands made.

Entering into the solitude of the games room, Benedict closed the door and strode toward the massive windows facing south. He pulled back the heavy damask drapery and stared out into the bleakness of the night. A decision had to be made and, when he returned to his room, he'd write several letters and send them posthaste. Two of his friends would receive instructions if anything suspicious were to happen to him and Estelle. Another letter would be sent to his father with promise of his return, and he'd also send a query to the Met asking for an opportunity to meet in privacy, off the earl's land and away from the deviants that lived in this abode.

If anything was certain, this family possessed the unique talent of putting on airs when there was very much awry. But one could suppose that summarization applied to all of aristocracy.

CHAPTER TEN

E stelle barely slept a wink. For as much as she wanted to jump into conversation with her fiancé, she could not put herself at ease. She sat up in bed, pondering the events of the last few days, attempting to assemble some sort of proper explanation for who instigated this entire intrigue and why, while Ben paced the room until her maid came knocking in the morning. Ben let her in, but promptly locked the door behind her.

"Oh, my!" Mary exclaimed. "This is definitely a scandal in the making. Lord St. John, you shouldn't be in here."

"I will leave and return shortly to escort Miss Humphrey down to breakfast. Be sure to lock the door behind me, and do not leave her alone. Not even for a second," Benedict ordered, rushing out of the room, but not before looking back at Estelle.

The maid nodded and locked the door behind him and turned to Estelle. "What has happened that he is most disturbed about?"

"I will explain later. Just help me into some clean clothing. I cannot believe I slept in this ensemble all night. I feel wretched, and I cannot breathe."

Her maid made quick work of unlacing the gown, and easing her out of the bustle skirt. Left in her chemise and stockings, Estelle fell back onto her bed and closed her eyes.

"Mary, what do you know of the manor's secrets and hidden passageways?" She felt the bed dip with the maid sitting next to her.

"I am not sure I understand your meaning, Miss. What secrets and hidden passageways?"

"I remember being specifically told that the new addition of the house had been added to reclaimed remnants of the old manor."

"Ah. Yes, now I know what you are talking about. The old wing that was salvaged is this one. The previous lord, Master Cuthbert's grandfather, had the manor restored, but died before he could move the family in. When my master became of age, he inherited the hall and the family has lived here ever since. As for secret passageways, the only one I know of is the old cellar."

"Where is that?"

"That's the tricky part, Miss. When this wing was rebuilt, they knocked out the wall and resealed the entire south side of the building. However, I did discover one day there's another entrance to the original lower level. I only happened upon the entrance as the cook asked me to go and fetch an herb from the garden last minute. I would even wager that to be the old kitchen in its day."

Hmm. An old lower level. I have to investigate. "Mary, how about you and I go for a stroll later? Pack a picnic basket with a little food, and be sure to pack a candle and matches. I feel compelled that we should go exploring."

"You're mad! Explore? After Evan scolding us over a tour? I highly disapprove."

"Yes, explore." Estelle wanted to tell her about the passage she found in her room, but considered against it. Whoever came into her room did not want to be found out, and if the deviant had been the same person who killed Gabriel, then it would be best to not give something they'd be able to use against Mary.

"On second thought, Mary, tell me how to get there, and I will go myself."

"I will not. You must have an escort, or I will not tell you at all."

Estelle began to lose her patience. "What if I have Ben come with me?"

"Would you really risk everything to learn this manor's secrets? If you do not mind my saying, Miss, I really think that it is probably best we never speak on this subject again. Now up with you, so I can finish dressing you. We have less than a half hour to get you ready for breakfast."

Estelle winced as her maid refastened her corset, and stepped away to pull down a fresh gown from the armoire.

It truly had to be a record time in getting dressed, yet she could not stop yawning. Breakfast would not only be a bore, but she could not fathom how she'd remain awake. Her mind travelled over to the discovery of the hidden passage behind the wall.

She caught herself glancing over to it for the tenth time in five minutes when the maid decided to comment.

"What is the matter, Miss? You have glared at the wall several times now."

"Uh…nothing is the matter, Mary. I am thinking after breakfast I might need a nap, but the room is too drafty. Do you think there is another room I can sleep in?"

"I have no idea, Miss. I will mention it to the head butler and see if anything can be done about it. Now off you go. You are ready, and if you pick up the pace, I daresay you might get there before Lady Cuthbert."

Estelle brushed off the idea of proper decorum and rushed out of her room, nearly knocking over a footman serving as valet for her fiancé. "My apologies. If I do not run, I will be late."

"Do not worry about a thing, Miss. Lady Cuthbert is dealing with a situation right now, and will be along a few minutes later than usual."

Down the hall and another flight of stairs, Estelle entered the already full breakfast room. Thankfully, her aunt had saved a seat between her and another guest, which unfortunately happened to be across from the earl's son.

When she sat down, a guest sitting next to George remarked on the countess's delay. "I cannot imagine what could be keeping her ladyship."

"My cousin, of course," George remarked snidely while sipping his coffee. "He is quite troubled, you know; tantrums, hissing. He is always angry and brooding over something bizarre. I have advised my father that our house simply isn't the proper place for a boy with those types of problems. A simpleton should be institutionalized."

"He will not!" the earl growled from the door. "He is upset, and over something you said, might I add. Once breakfast is over, you will join me in my library, George."

Estelle could not quite believe that no one in the room had risen from their seat, but they all soon followed suit once she did. When the earl and the countess finally sat at their respective seats, she overheard their hostess instruct a footman to have breakfast brought to Edwin's chambers.

She peered over to where Benedict sat and found him staring at the earl's son with a speculative glare. Lord, each passing day in this house was becoming stranger by the minute.

* * * *

Benedict tried to catch his fiancée sneaking out the back door, but did not get to her in time, before a maid stopped him.

"Excuse me, sir, Miss Humphrey thought you might need these things for your outing."

She handed him a basket and stood there as if waiting for a reply.

"What is all this?"

The maid leaned in and began to whisper, "The young miss hoped it would be a nice day for a picnic and a little exploration of the original portion of the building. She'll be waiting for you by the elm tree, a good ten yards from the service door here at the back."

"And please tell me, what exactly is the girl looking to discover?"

"I have no idea, but then again, I did tell her about the old kitchen area and cellar."

Old kitchen area and cellar? Why on earth would Estelle want to explore those areas?

"What did you tell her about that part of the house?"

"Not much, other than there's a secret passageway, or there had been one ages ago. You have to understand, I do not know what condition that part of the house is in. There was an easier way in, but when the master began renovations, the old wall had been removed and the only way in is through the cook's garden."

Benedict had to wonder what could possibly have fascinated his beloved to even consider traipsing into an old cellar. Yes, the passageway in her room was mysterious enough, but it was not at all sensible for a young woman to go snooping around an abandoned cellar either.

"Thank you very much, Mary. Is there anything else I should know about this cellar she is wanting to go looking in?"

She paused and tapped her chin thinking, and focused on him again. "I do not believe so. I suppose I should say to expect critters. It is not uncommon to find rats lying about, as well as those eight-legged demons. Lord, they are ever such disgusting creatures."

Benedict snorted. "I imagine Estelle will have much to say about those spiders. I suppose I should expect her to swoon at the first sight of one."

Mary snickered. "Well, if that doesn't teach her, I have no idea what would."

Benedict exited the main part of the house and strolled toward the elm tree where he found Estelle sitting patiently beneath, with her legs tucked neatly under her skirt. "Estelle, I have to say, your sense of adventure is bound to get us into trouble one of these days, if not thrown out of here."

She stared at him crossly. He could only imagine what she pondered in this precise moment. Benedict did not wish her ill, but her impulsiveness would certainly get them escorted off the property if they walked into something they weren't supposed to. He sat down next to her and took her hand into his, squeezing it gently.

"No matter what we find, Ben, I want to leave as soon as possible. I think I am quite done with all this intrigue. In fact, I have had enough of this family altogether. They're not right," she mumbled and then continued, "I do hope they'll move me. I do not think I can spend another night in a room knowing someone has access to it so freely."

"As I mentioned previously, I will ensure your room is changed. In fact, I will make sure your things are moved immediately in with your aunt. I do not want you alone, and this will ensure that you are always in the company of your chaperone. Now, what say we have a look in this basket and see what Mary has packed for us?" Benedict pulled away the cloth covering the items, revealing some bread, cheeses, and fruit. In addition, he found a candlestick and matches, assuming they were for their walk beneath the house.

The sound of someone carrying a conversation not far from them caught his attention. By now, Estelle had craned her neck and gazed into the field ahead of them. That was when he noticed her expression change to wide-eyed.

Estelle gasped and murmured lowly, "Is that the family's private cemetery? The ruins over there look like it might have been a chapel." She got up, brushing off the grass from her skirt and took the basket away from him.

"Estelle, what do you think you are doing?"

"Forget about the cellar. There's an adventure waiting to happen across the way. Come and let us see what is going on over there."

Heavens, the last thing Benedict wanted to do was to intrude on someone's privacy, but he did not think going to the cellar had been the right thing to do either. If following her to the family's cemetery kept Estelle from doing something illogical, then so be it. He would escort her, appeasing her curiosity and then they would return indoors, to where he would make the final arrangements for their departure.

* * * *

Estelle dragged her fiancé away as if he were a child in trouble. She knew all too well he would scold her afterwards, but she could not help but want to discover what exactly made this family so strange.

When they approached the newest headstone, a pang wrenched at her heart, rendering her speechless. The grave they had stopped at belonged to Helen. A lone tear dribbled down her cheek as she knelt down before the headstone. *Why does life have to be so unfair?*

Estelle thought back to that time in the perfumery, remembering word for word her friend's final words to her. Nothing made sense. She turned to talk to Ben only to find him walking amidst the other graves. A shiver licked up her spine, warning her that whatever had pushed Helen to get away from her family, the danger still loomed here at Hawthorne Hall. Although, she could not fathom what it could be.

"Estelle, come look at this," Ben called out to her, crouched down on his haunches. He held a crumpled up newspaper. He opened it when they heard laughter echoing nearby.

"Did you hear that?" she asked before taking the paper out of his hand. About to open and read the partial periodical, the laughter commenced again. "Where do you think it is coming from Ben? I cannot see from here."

"My guess is the crypt just ahead of us. Wait," Ben whispered before clamping his hand over her mouth. I think I hear someone coming."

Estelle removed his hand and scowled. The man had no business to silence her in such a manner. She leaned over to peer around another stone, and watched the earl's son look in their direction but did not notice their presence. He then turned toward the cook's garden and disappeared behind a trellis.

That has to be the way to the cellar.

Estelle returned her focus to her betrothed, grasping hold of his lapels. "We should follow where the laughter came from, Ben. Whatever is going on, I am pretty sure we'll be able to figure out what has got to be a connection to Helen."

"Are you certain, my dear? I cannot bear the thought of something terrible happening to you. Truth be told, Estelle, I think we should head on back to the house." He rose to his feet, pulling her up as well.

She did not want to head back to the house. Estelle desired to get to the bottom of this terrifying intrigue, but the estate terrified her just as equally. Estelle proceeded into the crypt, following the walls as a guide until Ben lit the candle behind her, illuminating the way before them.

"This is quite unusual, Ben. I did not think they still made crypts."

"Judging by the carvings and the stonework, I imagine this had been built over a hundred years ago, dearest. What I would like to know is whose voice did we hear laughing in here, and if they did not leave through the entrance then there has to be a hidden passage."

Estelle leaned against the back wall, resting her arm on a statue, releasing a wall and exposing a set of stairs going down. She turned toward Benedict, who grumbled quietly,

"Another blasted passageway."

"You go first, Ben. I am starting to think this might have been a mistake."

He went on ahead of her down a winding, narrow staircase. At the bottom they encountered two different dirt lined paths. One appeared to lead toward the direction of the ruins of what could have been a chapel, and the other was unknown. But that was when they heard the laughter again.

Ben had put his arm out to keep her from moving forward, and turned his head. "My dear, are you sure you want to do this? There will be no going back if we find ourselves in trouble. Who is to say we may not make it back to the house?"

Estelle scowled and pushed his arm away. "I did not realize you were such a coward, Ben."

He put the basket down, and turned to face her. "This is not me displaying cowardice, Estelle. This is me recommending that we're sensible in how we proceed. Not to mention, if we find ourselves in any kind of trouble, how do you think this is going to look to our hosts?"

"Fine. We will travel a bit further, but then we will turn back."

This time Ben scowled at her. "No, Estelle. I have to put my foot down. We will head back to the house now. When we return, I will ensure that you are moved into your aunt's room and will look at arranging a passage home for you ladies. Besides, I have been given some news to give to my father, and I would like to get that finished immediately."

Frustration mounted, and Estelle wanted nothing more than to scream. How dare he tell her what to do, and the mere mention of leaving her with her aunt while he went away on business annoyed her immensely.

Estelle followed him out of the crypt into the cemetery and back toward the house from the entrance they had left in. In a small way, she was glad that they left at his insistence, but not finding out who laughed pricked her curiosity.

Just as they closed the door behind them, their host found them in the hall.

"Ah, there you are, Miss Humphrey. I hope the fresh air did you some good. You will be happy to know that Mary has moved your things to your aunt's room. I imagine you'll find the arrangement more to your liking."

"Thank you kindly, my lord. I hope it was not too much of an inconvenience."

"Nonsense. You should have told me sooner that you found the room too drafty." Clucking his tongue, the earl turned to Benedict, "Lord St. John, would you care to join me in my billiards room? I think I have come up with a solution to my problem that we discussed earlier."

Ben glanced at her and bowed his head.

She took that as her cue to leave and perhaps find her aunt. Her chaperone might be wanting an explanation as to why she wanted to share a room with her. She took off in the direction of the main foyer and the earl's son leaning against the railing of the stairs.

"I wondered when I would see you around. I had heard that you changed rooms. I am sorry you did not find the room comfortable." "My lord—" Estelle curtsied.

"Call me George."

"Well, George. The room was a wee bit on the drafty side. Considering my wedding is only a month away, I would hate to catch the death of me," she said barely cracking a smile, desperately trying not to give away that they'd discovered the passageway.

"Are you truly pleased to be marrying Lord St. John? I know many a woman who marry to save them from dastardly situations. Besides, I have heard that if things don't improve that his fortune will suffer, and the entirety of his family including you—will be reduced to nothing more than commoners. Do you not come from a family that has ties to English and French aristocracy?"

"I fail to comprehend how my ancestry is relevant to your inquisition, my lord."

How in the world did he know so much about her personal and family life? She did not recall ever mentioning it before today. Besides, what business was it of his who she married and why?

He smirked and his eyes danced with some plot he hadn't revealed yet.

"Last I recall, my lord, I have never, ever given any indication my pending nuptials to Lord St. John were of the convenient sort. Nor, are we marrying because of an improper liaison. And if you must know, I love him with all my heart. I care not for his supposed lacking connections due to poor choices his papa might have made, as I personally find them cumbersome, and a hindrance of true potential. While many are born privileged, it is those same titles that keep people from finding true happiness, and sometimes greed changes a person. Now, if you do not mind, I need to find my aunt." He waved a hand before her as if he had to give her permission to pass.

She could not believe the audacity he had, to imply she would not be satisfied with Ben. The nerve. If anything, it was as plain as day their host and his countess did not demonstrate a keen affection for each other. All appearances led her to believe their situation had been of the convenient sort. This, in her fine opinion, spoke volumes on the values they placed on life and those around them.

This sentiment then led her to wonder why any of them were invited to this home in the first place. Most of the guests in attendance had nothing in common; no connections to the family, except for Ben. His father worked for the earl for fifteen years now, and did not have much to show for it, other than a family he cared deeply for.

Even her family—while it had its ties to nobility—when her father married her mother those ties had been severed. All over a family feud and marrying someone out of their class. As it were, she had never seen her parents argue in all her years. So whatever connections they lost, her parents had a deep affection, as it should be.

CHAPTER ELEVEN

Benedict held the billiards cue, awaiting what his host had to say, anticipating his earlier comment in reference to Edwin. Another gentleman had joined them in the room, looking on their setup. Not that he minded if they had company, but he would have figured that the earl would prefer to keep this discussion private.

Benedict wondered what kind of plan he had for the troubled young man. Did he anticipate there would be resistance? Who knew? The mere fact that the earl had mentioned that his nephew had been upset over something George had said, left him curious. Clearly the boy was sensitive to a fault, and whether or not his sister's or his parents' deaths contributed to the problem, the only way to find out was to engage the young man further.

"So, what is this solution you mentioned, my lord?"

"Lord Haverford dropped by shortly after breakfast and mentioned that his gardener is in need of an extra hand. While I would still like for you to source out some employment for Edwin, would you mind visiting Lord Haverford's gardener and find out if the boy would be truly suited for the employment?"

While Benedict did not mind giving the earl a hand, he had to wonder when he became his man of affairs. Perhaps now was a good time to request his leave in delivering the message to his father.

Benedict sunk a ball in a pocket, while another strayed away in the opposite direction. The earl raised his eyebrow and gazed at him with speculation.

"Not bad, sir. Lord St. John, you are quite adept at demonstrating your precision."

"Thank you, my lord. Believe me when I say, I have had plenty of practice."

The earl chuckled and leaned against the table. "You look like a man who has much going on in his mind. Why not share your troubles with me, and I will see what I can do to help?"

"No trouble at all actually. Now that Estelle has been moved into her aunt's room, we are both satisfied. However, the only thing is, I do need to leave for a few days to head back to town on business. I wonder if it isn't a huge imposition that the ladies remain here until I make arrangements for their return home?"

His host laughed heartily and walked toward him, placing a firm grip on his shoulder. "It would never be an imposition. The ladies are safe and welcome to stay here. I should also add, I thank you for the return of the book. My wife sometimes…I wish she were mute. Her constant whining and complaining drove me mad for days over such a silly thing."

"I cannot thank you enough for your patience and understanding. I will be departing at daybreak, and I would prefer that you do not go into too many details in the event anyone asks."

"Not to worry, my friend. As it happens, most of the guests are departing tomorrow, and I believe your lovely fiancée and her aunt will be kept company by Baron Milton and his wife."

Benedict could not have been more pleased with the news they would not be alone with this crazed family. Now all he had to do was post a note to the inspector from Scotland Yard—as he had his own questions—and another to his father, advising him of his imminent arrival. Besides, there was much to be completed with the wedding and this last minute visitation took up some of the time they needed for their planning.

He didn't even have the opportunity to book their passage to France. It was his wedding gift to her, well, that and her papa and aunt insisted on paying for half, but he wanted that last little detail to remain silent. Estelle would have objected to her family aiding them on their trip. He could hear her now. *Ben, how could you! We should have saved the money for something else. I cannot believe my father and aunt would encourage such a costly adventure.* Yes, she would be cross, but he would make up for the expensive trip in other ways. He was committed to spending his life showing her just how much he loved her.

Speaking of which, he needed to find her and see how the arrangement with the room was coming along.

The earl concluded the game, sinking the remaining three balls, chuckling with his success. "Why, shall we all move into the library for some drinks? I'm parched."

Benedict bowed his head and stared his host in the eye. "While I would like nothing more than to join you, I suppose I should put my things together for my departure tomorrow. Estelle and her aunt will want to know of my plans."

"Very well, young man, perhaps you'll join me after dinner."

Benedict was the first to leave the billiards room and followed the hall until he reached the stairs. About to head forward, he paused at the sound of some whispers around the corner.

"If it weren't for you, none of this would have happened."

"Your parents are idiots for celebrating the biggest sham ever born in England. If they really knew your true character…you…you—"

"Quit your sniveling, you poor excuse for a man. If you had not gone to her room, none of this would have been an issue. But, no, did you listen? Why would you listen to a mastermind of deception? You should have killed yourself long ago. There's time yet though. Mark my words. Do not be surprised if the Met learns who set the cottage on fire. Last I heard they had left the case open."

Just what in the world were the earl's son and nephew going on about? He'd have to ask about a further detailed background on the two when he sat down with the inspector.

Benedict had heard enough. Refusing to listen to any more nonsense, he ascended the stairs, continuing on to visit with his travelling companions. He stopped outside their door and knocked several times before Estelle's aunt opened the door.

"Lord St. John; how nice of you to join us. We just rang for tea. I hope you will accompany us."

"I think I will, but only for a short while. I thought I would take some time and see how you ladies are faring."

Estelle's aunt ushered him in, offering him a seat at the round table between the window and the fireplace, their view the north side of the property and where they had spent part of the morning outdoors at the cemetery. In fact, anyone who had a room on this side of the house would have been able to see it clearly.

He could see the crypt off in the distance, and the crumbling remains of what could have been a chapel. Benedict also was able to see part of the garden, as he watched the cook and one of the kitchen help rifling through the garden's contents. He could not help but wonder who else had a room in this wing, and who might have seen them. If anyone did indeed see them venturing off in an area they weren't supposed to, they could soon find themselves booted off the property.

"Tell me, ladies, who else has a room in this wing?"

Estelle looked at him, perplexed. "I have no idea. Although, now that you mention it, I thought I heard some maids leaving a room at the end of the hall and referred to it as the master's room. I doubt that it came from the earl's room. One would have to assume they were either making reference to George or Edwin." *Interesting.*

After happening upon their conversation at the bottom of the stairs, their whispering led him to conclude those two were up to mischief. Benedict had a sneaking suspicion that the earl's nephew might be the one who used the secret passage-way in his fiancée's room, but how could he prove it? Nevertheless, he would go over his suspicions with the inspector and see what they could find out.

As far as he deduced, the lot could not be trusted. Before he left, he had to catch Edwin alone and see how much he knew of his uncle's plan for him. But first, he had to post a letter right away.

"Well, my dears, I should probably tell you I need to leave for a day or two at daybreak. I will be arranging for a coach to pick you up and take you to London."

"Must you go so soon? Why can we not travel with you, Ben?" Estelle whined.

He could see the hint of fear in her eyes.

Her aunt looked at him sympathetically. "Quit that childish behavior, Estelle. Lord St. John obviously has business that requires attention. My dear boy, if you must, then do what is necessary. And do not worry about the arrangements. I am quite capable of organizing a coach myself."

"While that is not necessary, I do appreciate your offer. No, just leave it to me. On that note, ladies, I think I will head to my room now and send word to my father regarding my departure. As it turns out, the earl wishes for his son to take over the business of managing the accounts and the family's various estates. He has requested my father to train the boy, so I reckon it best I give him a bit of warning."

Both ladies scowled at him like he had magically grown another head.

"I know exactly what you are both thinking, and I agree. The earl has made it clear that he plans to compensate my father well, and provide him with an excellent reference. However, I can see what his motivation was in inviting us here this week. If that was not strange enough, I have been requested to find his nephew employment. Apparently, he doesn't want the lad here anymore, and I suspect there is more to the story than he is divulging."

"That is quite odd. If the boy is troubled like he implied at breakfast, no employer in their right mind would consider him," Estelle added.

Benedict knew the challenge ahead of him would test him sorely, but what choice did he have in the matter? Ever since that blissful evening when Estelle appeared in his room, he had relieved himself every night. He longed to hold her, but knew all too well, the proper thing would be to wait.

He entered his room and found it in complete disarray. His personal belongings were strewn across the floor. Benedict supposed that nothing would surprise him at this point, yet the moment he discovered a dismembered finger placed on his pillow, his hands trembled. Heat flushed through his body, and his pulse raced. Benedict couldn't remember the last time he'd be this furious.

When will this madness ever end?

Benedict rang for a servant, who swiftly appeared in the chamber. "How can I be of assistance, sir?"

"Well, for starters, you can remove this finger and replace the pillow at once. Oh, and you might as well summon his lordship, too. This has gone far enough."

"Y—yes, sir. Right away, my lord."

Benedict had been tempted to tidy up the mess himself, but thought against the matter. He did a turn around the room, scouring it for clues as to who might have been there, until he came across a note strategically placed on the mantle of the fireplace; he reached for it and read it aloud.

I know what you are planning. Consider this a warning. You are next.

"Good God, man! What happened here?" the earl questioned, walking deeper into his room.

"Did your servant explain a finger had been placed on my pillow, and I just found this note?" Benedict passed the note to the earl and awaited his reply. Only he did not get one. Instead, his lordship tossed the card into the low burning fire.

Benedict's eyes widened, and the sudden urge to yell rose to the surface. "Why in God's name did you destroy the evidence?"

He never got a response. When a servant returned with a clean pillow, the earl interjected. "Do not worry about the pillow, William. Have Lord St. John moved immediately into Helen's old room. We shall address this mess afterwards. I do hope you understand, my lord. I will take care of this matter myself. There is no need to summon for the constable as I know who the culprit is, and will see to it immediately."

Before Benedict could question him anymore, the earl had departed with haste, and by the time he turned around to the servant, his things were already collected and put in his trunk. He did not like the idea of spending the night in the room that included a secret passage. It was a ludicrous thought, and all the better they were leaving in the morning.

William arranged his belongings and after setting a fire and preparing the bed, he left him alone. Within minutes, Benedict had crawled into bed and closed his eyes. He had not realized how much energy being angry and frustrated utilized.

* * * *

Estelle waited eagerly for her beloved to come and escort her to dinner, but when a heavy knock at her chamber door alarmed her, she was most disappointed to see Edwin frantic, and with his hands fisted at his sides.

"May I come in? I have something urgent I must talk to you about."

"This is most irregular, sir. Does your uncle know you are here?" her aunt questioned behind her.

Estelle could not very well leave the man standing in the hall. "Come in. Can I get you a drink of water?"

"No. I cannot stay very long. The earl has forbidden me to interact with his guests, but I will keep this meeting brief." He paused and took a wary glance at Estelle. He appeared worried and terribly troubled. Edwin paced the room at a speed that would have normally left grooves in the floorboards.

Pity flooded her emotions, as she did not think the man capable of harming a fly, when he stopped in front of the window and began to whisper.

"He knows that you know, Miss Humphrey. You must leave as soon as you can. He is a sinful fool, the devil's incarnate. He cannot be trusted, and for as long as you are here, he will ruin you."

"What on earth are you talking about, Edwin? Who knows what?"

His eyes widened just as Ben opened her door. "The secret passageway in the bedroom and the crypt. I must leave. I have said too much."

Her aunt waved her hand. "Lord St. John, how kind of you to join us. Estelle has some disturbing news to share with you."

Edwin dashed out of the room, leaving them both bereft. *Who knows? Dash it. I want to know.* Whoever it was though, knew of hers and Ben's impromptu trip to the graveyard and the crypt. Estelle pondered on this for a moment, supposing it would only be a matter of time before their host found out.

"Dare I ask why in God's name that boy would even hazard the chance in coming to our room if he knew something was amiss?" Aunt Margaret asked, scowling as she took a seat at the edge of her bed.

"Apparently, the earl's nephew has got it in his head that someone—whoever it is— knows about us knowing about the secret passage, and a crypt."

"What in damnation are you talking about, Estelle? Did you stumble across a passageway or crypt? I am not sure I can take much more of this nonsense."

"Auntie, I did discover a hidden passage in the room I was assigned. That is the reason why Ben insisted I stay with you."

"My, oh my. Has our host been informed of this? This is a violation of privacy and I will not tolerate such insolence. Something must be done this instant," her aunt added, quite put out by this sudden information. "As it turns out, Estelle, the Baron Egerton and his wife will be leaving tomorrow after breakfast. I suggested that they take us along on their return to town. The baroness is quite agreeable, so I hope you do not mind my interfering, Estelle."

Estelle then turned to her fiancé. The hard lines around his mouth and eyes noted something more than passing concern. His body language emanated a noticeable yet silent fear. Had something happened to him too? She wished that this awkward moment of silence would pass.

"Estelle…"

"They know that we know."

"Ah, well, I just recently discovered that myself. How did you find out?"

"The earl's nephew," Estelle whispered, in fear that someone would hear them discussing this matter.

Ben glared at her aunt and offered her a reassuring smile. "We will let the matter rest for now. Dinner is about to be served and with all of us departing on the morrow, with any luck we will never have to think about this confounded place ever again." "Indeed," her aunt added.

"Now, can I see to the pleasure of escorting you fine ladies to dinner?"

For the first time during their journey, Estelle could not help but feel excitement washing over her. They would finally be leaving, all of them. Estelle took her fiancé's arm and smiled cheerfully as he led her and her aunt to the dining hall. On their way to the dining room, they passed a footman.

"Did my letters make the evening post?" Benedict asked.

"Yes, Lord St. John. I imagine they will arrive right on time."

"Most excellent, my good man. Have the others arrived in the dining hall?"

"No, sir. I do not believe his lordship and the countess have arrived. Neither have Edwin or George. The only people already seated are the baron, the baroness, and Lords Duncan and Beecham."

Ben nodded and they continued to follow his lead until they entered the room. The table had been done up most elegantly and candles illuminated the room, so much so that their shadows danced on the brocade draped walls. Liveried footmen waited along the one side of the wall before taking their positions from the butler.

Arriving at their seats, all the guests stood up and waited for them to be seated. Only to then stand up again once their hosts arrived in the room. Once everyone was seated, his lordship decided to put on airs like nothing had ever happened during their stay at the manor. In fact, he appeared too cheerful.

"I suppose it is only natural seeing as most of you will be departing tomorrow— albeit at different times—we considered a proper send-off was in order. The countess has ordered a most excellent dinner and we hope that everyone enjoys it." The earl clinked the crystal glass before him and more uniformed footmen came through with platters.

In all reality, tonight would be the last time that she, her aunt, and Ben would dine in such a stately manner. Come to think of it, she could not imagine if there would ever be another opportunity.

The room filled with conversation until the countess shrieked and swooned in her seat. All eyes were on the earl's wife, who slumped in her chair while a maid fanned her, and the earl rushed over to see what happened.

"Do not just stand there. Call for the physician." He lifted his wife out of the seat, happening to glance at the platter before her. A bloodied finger had been strategically placed in the lamb's mouth. He then glared at a nearby footman, who stood there aghast at the horror. "You, remove that blasted platter. I will be back shortly. I will see to taking the countess to her room. Where in God's name is my son?" he bellowed, raging out of the hall.

So much for a quiet and joyful evening. The guests for certain would all be sleeping with one eye open.

CHAPTER TWELVE

Benedict could not even begin to fathom how upset the earl must have been. All the gentlemen had been gathered in the library now for an hour, waiting on their host to return from his wife's room.

None of the men, including him, had even seen the earl's heir and nephew. By now, either one or both would have made an appearance. He could not understand how two grown men behaved like boys, even in the presence of company. How he looked forward to looking deeper into the family's history.

The earl did not enter the library until half past nine, and by then some of the men had already retired. Duncan remained behind, but lord only knew he grew impatient by the second.

"Has no one seen my son? I have looked all over this damned house, and he is nowhere to be found."

"What was that, my lord? Why would you want to speak to me after that sound scolding you gave me this morning? You might as well have called a priest, you might learn a thing or two on delivering a sermon," George added dryly from the doorway.

"You insolent fool. Of all the children that survived, I had to be stuck with you for an heir. Heaven forbid—"

Benedict could not help but feel awkward and out of place.

Duncan nudged him and then leaned in to whisper, "If I have not said it before, I am telling you again. This family has trouble. I have a sneaking suspicion the worst is yet to come."

"Where is your blasted cousin? I have not been able to locate him either," the earl asked.

"How should I know? The ungrateful brat is always taking off when he is upset."

The earl mumbled something and stepped away from his son, and walked toward his favorite chair. A footman waiting nearby poured Lord Cuthbert a drink, and, after passing it to him, he stepped back, awaiting more orders.

"I think it is rather clear that every time I think things could not get worse a body shows up, or dismembered appendages. I cannot imagine what the inspector will have to say about this."

"My lord, a man can very well survive without a finger. We cannot assume there is another body, that is, until it is found," Benedict advised, taking a nearby seat, and his friend followed suit. "I realize this is all very troubling, but I am certain you will get to the bottom of this," he advised angrily while he fisted his hands.

Benedict leaned back in his seat, pulling out his pocket watch. He had to retire early, or he would never make it out on time to head back to town. "Well, gentlemen, I think I will retire for the evening. My lord, I will look into those things tomorrow as you requested."

As he walked by George, he heard him mumble, "We will see about that."

Benedict could not believe what he heard, so when he turned his head to glare at the earl's son, the insolent fool snickered.

"A good evening to you, Lord St. John. I am ever grateful that you could attend this week."

Benedict left the room with Duncan following him out as well. Duncan was right; the worst was yet to come.

* * * *

"Estelle, what are you reading?"

Oh, mama, how I wish you were still here. I fear for my life. Edwin has become unstable. I overheard the servants the other night commenting on his frequent trips into the Limehouse District. Just yesterday, Matthew had to retrieve him at the request of my dear uncle. Edwin is in such a state that he stormed into the library and began throwing things. Our uncle, of course, is quite vexed and has forbidden him to leave the manor.

Then there is George. He visited my room last night, and this time I caught him coming through a sliding panel near my bed. George did not realize I could see him entering, but I kept my eyes closed.

Oh, how I wish Gabriel could speak with my uncle sooner. If we could run away and marry by way of the blacksmith, I know he'd keep me safe.

I am not sure how much more I can take of this. Do I risk my soul ending up in purgatory if I put an end to this, or do I allow them both to destroy me until there is nothing left? A child cannot be born from these relations. I have to find a way to get away. I am so lost…

Mama, why did you leave me?

Benedict had caught her unawares in the parlor, looking jittery and on the verge of weeping. She fumbled with the final letter Helen wrote, days before she was found dead.

"Are you reading one of the romantic poems you love to read? Wait, why do you look weepy? What is the matter? If you are truly unhappy here,

I will arrange for us to leave right away," he admonished.

"You cannot leave," George said from the doorway. "I mean, that is to say, with the officers now gone, we can be at ease. The Mr. Templeton will have a proper funeral and all."

"Is there any other reason for your interruption, George?" Estelle asked, moving closer to her fiancé.

"No, I will be on my way now." He glared at her sardonically. George walked out without so much as giving them a second look.

Estelle had not meant to come across as rude, but she did not want to be left alone with him. After reading Helen's stack, being under the same roof with Edwin and George was not safe. "Ben, we need to leave as soon as possible. When we return to town, I have something to give to the inspector."

"What is it, Estelle?"

"I found letters, evidence that things are not what they seem to be. No one is safe here, not even us. We need to leave and try and stop this before anyone else dies."

He gripped her arms and gave her a discerning look. "If you know who murdered Gabriel, you need to tell me, now."

"I know who murdered Gabriel, and I am pretty sure I know what happened to Helen. But I will not tell you while we are here. We must leave. I will not stay here any longer than necessary."

Estelle felt the weight of her worries lift from her chest. She followed Benedict out of the parlor and found the maid that showed her to the attic.

"Mary, would you come along with us? I need a hand with some packing."

"Yes, ma'am. Allow me to get word to our driver."

Estelle followed her beloved up the stairs to her room, only to open the door and find her room had been ransacked.

"What in damnation!" Ben bellowed behind her, nearly knocking her over as he rushed into the room. "What could you possibly have that would warrant this mess?"

When their host joined them, Lord Cuthbert gasped and he blanched at the condition of the room. "I had heard you were leaving, and I can certainly see why. The bizarre events these last few days are disturbing."

"You cannot tell me that this is surprising, Lord Cuthbert. I imagine since Helen and her brother arrived here, things began happening," Estelle said.

The earl did not respond, so she continued grilling him. "And you cannot be remiss in what truly happened to Helen. Her death is no mystery at all, admit it; she took her own life."

He grimaced, but then spoke softly. "She did, though I do not know why. She always seemed so happy, very pleasant to be around people. Her passing was quite tragic. Things have not been quite the same. Her brother went into a decline, and our own George could not stand to be under the same roof. After Helen's death, he went on a tour of the continent. He took it so hard, he needed time away." *I am sure he did.*

"I have taken too much of your time already. Thank you for joining our family here, Lord St. John, Miss Humphrey." The earl bowed and left them to her packing.

She could not wait to be at home with her papa and continue finalizing her wedding plans.

CHAPTER THIRTEEN

Two days later.

"Estelle, you have a visitor," her papa said.

"Please tell me it is Ben."

"I wish I could, dearest, but it is not. I believe it is an inspector from Scotland Yard."

Scotland Yard? "Show him in, Papa, and I would be happy to answer any questions the gentleman might have."

A man slightly shorter than Ben entered the room. He wore spectacles, and his cheeks were a ruddy color. Portly in stature, he had to be nearing fifty in age. The gentleman took a seat across from her and studied her for a moment. He coughed and then opened his notebook. "Miss Humphrey, it is my understanding that you and Lord St.

John are engaged. Is this fact true?"

"It is. We are to be married in two weeks' time."

"And when was the last time you saw Lord St. John?"

"The night before we left Lord Cuthbert's estate, sir. I sent word to his home, but I have not heard anything back. I would be lying if I said I was not worried."

The inspector paused to write something down and continued, "Miss Humphrey, were you aware that he sent me a missive during your stay at Hawthorne Hall, advising he was highly suspicious of your host's family? He had some concerns and wanted to express them to me in person. 'Tis the truth. I have been waiting for him to arrive at my station for the same amount of time. Would you have any reason to suspect that the Cuthbert's would do anything to harm him?"

"No but on the eve of our departure, there had been an incident at the dinner table. Apparently, the countess had a platter placed in front of her, and in the mouth of the lamb a freshly dismembered finger stuck out. There is also the questionable death of Mr. Gabriel Templeton, who supposedly threw himself onto the terrace. " She paused to look at her papa and returned her attention to the inspector again. "Ben also found a dismembered finger on his pillow."

His eyebrows shot up, and a gasp from the door alerted her that her aunt had been listening in.

"Be honest with me, young lady. Have there been any more deaths since that first night you arrived? Your fiancé told me about your swoon that night, after that gent fell to his death from the terrace. Do you have any reason to suspect someone from the house pushed him?"

Estelle pondered, but knew too little of the family's history to suspect they would be capable of any wrong-doing.

"No. I cannot say that I know any of them that well. However, before the earl's niece, Helen, passed away so suddenly, she was planning to get away to the country. At least that is what she confided in me. We had been friends for a while, you see. She wouldn't confide in me why, but it was clear there had been a matter of distrust between her and George. I cannot even say if he is the reason why she wanted to leave."

"My dear, the only single reason why a girl would swiftly retreat to the country, is if she were with child. I am going to tell you a little secret about the Cuthbert's. They are a lot of sinners. Helen's death had been poorly covered up, and by the time I had just enough evidence to bring in

George for questioning, the earl had paid off the magistrate, and case closed. If I had to stake my life on it, I am certain that George had his hands on her."

An incestuous affair? The inspector has to be wrong. He just has to be. Why would the earl's son even consider such a sinful act? Although at this point nothing would surprise her.

"I know this is not the appropriate time to mention this, but it might be useful in your current investigation. The night I swooned, I was returned to my room. I had been drugged and later told that a red rose tied with a black ribbon had been left on my bed. Several days later, we discovered a secret passageway into my room. You should know if there is one, there has to be more, although I cannot confirm it."

The inspector closed his notebook and glanced at her with wary eyes. "I think that your information will help. However, we still have the issue of your missing fiancé. Even his parents haven't heard from him, and he was expected around the same time. If I have need for you to return with me, will you?"

"Absolutely not!" her father bellowed from the door. "I will not let her return to that devil's home. Not after everything she has revealed." Her papa turned his focus on her now. "My dear, sweet girl, why did you not tell me? Your foolish aunt should have informed me the instant you both returned."

Estelle had pleaded with her aunt for thirty minutes before they arrived home; it had much to do with her parents being uninformed of the tragedy during their visitation.

The inspector got up from his seat and inclined his head toward her. "I thank you kindly for your time, Miss Humphrey. I will see myself out."

He rose and strode to the door slowly and then stopped, as if remembering something. The inspector turned around and faced her once again. "Just one last note, Miss. The earl's heir returned to England under suspicious motives. His original plans were to return one month from tomorrow, and I have it on good authority that I am to expect French officials any day now. Do you think George Cuthbert is capable of murder?"

Estelle's stomach dropped somewhere beneath her feet. Could it really have been George this entire time? Inconceivable to think the man acted alone. He had to have an accomplice. Yet, the inspector stood there waiting for an answer.

"Estelle, dearest, do not keep the man waiting. I am certain he would like to get home in time for his supper," her aunt drawled.

"I apologize, Inspector, but if I had to guess, and after everything that has transpired at the manor thus far, I would have to confirm that your suspicions would not be a far stretch of the truth."

"Thank you, Miss, Mr. Humphrey."

I cannot believe I just had this discussion.

* * * *

Benedict shook his head, waiting for the fog to lift and his senses to return. He'd been bound to a post, and his limited vision from the darkness didn't help one bit.

Damnation! What happened?

The scent of rotting wood and decaying flesh burned his nasal passages, and the floor he sat upon dampened his trousers. Just where in the world was he, and how? *Blast it. George!*

But where had George taken him? At what remote location did he have him concealed, or did he dare to return him to the estate? The last memory he had was being hit over the head, which explained the blasted pain throbbing in his skull. Nausea made him want to heave but he continued to keep breathing at a steady pace.

Benedict tried to recount all the events that led to where he sat. His friend had fallen from the terrace the first night, then someone entered Estelle's room via a secret passageway and

drugged her. Not one but two fingers were con-
veniently placed on a dinner platter and on his
pillow. There were far too many inconsistencies
with all the different attacks.

Benedict started to believe there was more
than one assailant, which disturbed him on a
greater scale. Just what in the world were the
Cuthbert's protecting?

A noise somewhere off in the distance alerted
him that he would not be alone for much longer.
Benedict tried to calm himself, but soon found his
imagination running away on him.

"Look who is finally awake." Darkness en-
gulfed him, and only the light from the lantern that
George had brought with him gave him a little
hope.

"Why am I here, George? Or are you afraid
that the inspector is going to dig deeper?"

"Silence!" George bellowed, his voice echoing
in their cavernous surroundings.

Benedict heard a moaning somewhere behind
him. Who could possibly be in here with him? He
tried to crane his neck, but George delivered him
a blow to the face.

"Leave him be. He went into shock after I cut
off the second finger. He'll survive. Maybe not. I
have not quite decided what to do with the imp.

He had a most unnatural obsession with his sister; hasn't been quite right in the head since the bloody day she died. It is just as well he should join sweet Helen." George had stepped away from the light, kicking the dirt with his boots. "You should know after this, I cannot let you live. It would be supremely stupid of me to leave any evidence behind."

"So were you the one."

"George, where are you, you bloody idiot!" his father called from outside.

The cellar! This must have been the confounded place the maid had previously mentioned to Estelle.

"Keep silent." George ran over to his cousin and covered his mouth, muffling the moans of agony from his disfigured hand, and aimed his gun at Benedict.

Long moments passed before another word could be heard beyond their hiding place. He wondered if he had been dragged to that very place Estelle had wanted to explore— the cellar—beneath the original portion of the home. But how in the world had he dragged him in here without anyone noticing? Did someone aid him?

Not that any of it mattered at this point; at the end of the day, he knew precisely what his fate was, and going home to Estelle didn't appear to be it. How he longed to see her one last time; her long, dark hair unraveled and spilling over his pillow, her soft curves wrapped in nothing but his arms in his bed. That first night that they had shared minimal intimacy made him crave her more, and now he could smell the soft lavender scent that she wore. Her dark eyes would never burrow into his soul, and he would have to wait until she met her time in the afterlife before they saw each other again.

Benedict knew his mental ramblings were a little on the dramatic side—Shakespeare might have been proud—but he desperately hoped for a small opportunity for him to get free.

Edwin's moaning ceased after he heard what sounded like a crack. *Good grief. Had the earl's heir slammed the boy's head against the wall?* He wondered why the earl never entered where they were being held captive either. The possibility of the arse being involved with his abduction was highly probable, yet explained so much. George approached him, snickering all the while.

"He will come to soon enough. He cannot possibly come out of it more addled than what he was to begin with. Now then, let us have a little chat about the note you were meaning to send to

London." George paused and crouched down to his haunches and smirked. The lantern behind him cast an eerie shadow of his profile on the river-rock wall, and Ben could now see the decayed carcasses of rats and other field creatures strewn apart. Had this cellar been a hiding place where they practiced mutilating living things?

"I understand that the earl is relieving your father's man from his duties, and he expects me to take over. The sorry fact of the matter is, I care not for his fortune and would rather this home be burnt to the ground with its inhabiting ghosts. Our family has had a rather long history of murder. Did you know? And as far as my father's accounts go, the earl knows nothing of my own fortune I acquired on my travels." *Murder?*

"I have no idea what you are talking about," Benedict replied with a speculative gaze.

"What is this? The all-knowing Lord St. John has not educated himself in our scandalous family history? Let me see if I can remember it all." He paused and sat on his backside across from him. "My father has killed countless men in duels, and I do believe a scuffle at a gentlemen's club last year. Apparently, the sod he fist-cuffed was found floating face down in the Thames. Then there is Edwin, who all but burnt the family's Scottish country home, taking his mother and father to the devil. Sweet, sweet Helen had been fortunate enough to be finishing her last term at school. I believe that was when I recognized she'd lost her bloom."

Benedict contemplated the boy's expressions. The moment he began to discuss his cousin Helen, he had the lustful glaze men had when they were pensive of a lover they favored. He'd wondered if it were a mutual affection too, for Helen would have certainly seen his true colors by then and turned him away.

"I can tell you are exasperated with my news. I can say my mother is no saint either. So, now do you understand why I say this place is just better if it had burnt down to the ground? One is certain in all this madness that surrounds us; no one will live to tell about it. That is my final promise to everyone who still remains in this house."

"Do you mean to tell me that you plan to harm everyone, including the house servants?"

George snorted and rose from the ground. He paced the floor with his hands folded back, muttering under his breath and looking toward the entrance of the abandoned cellar. "Well, I guess I am off. Father will be tearing through the house looking for Edwin and I.

Rest easy tonight knowing it will be your last."

The earl's son departed, taking the lantern with him and not saying another word.

Benedict did have one thing to his advantage; the fool had no idea of the note he had sent earlier to the inspector. *With any luck, the inspector will realize I'm missing, and return to the house.*

* * * *

Edwin writhed with pain, unsure if he would die from the blow to his head. His body ached like nothing before. His thoughts were jumbled with things of the past and future. It had not occurred to him just how deviant George was until the rogue had divulged what he had done to the French lady he left behind. The French authorities couldn't come fast enough to whisk this idiot away.

A strangled cough only a few feet away from him alerted him he was not alone, until he overheard the whispered name of Estelle. Good God. George had captured Lord St. John. Did his madness know no boundaries? Sooner or later the Peelers, family, and friends, would descend upon Hawthorne Hall in search of him. How he wished that time were now, but as it were, Edwin was beginning to doubt they would live another day.

"Wake up, St. John. Wake up," he called out but the man continued to mumble.

They were doomed. He should have set this manor ablaze when he had the opportunity to do so. All this trouble, murder, deceit would have been avoided had he listened to his instincts.

CHAPTER FOURTEEN

Estelle entered the hidden passage in the cellar. The dark, dank smell of the foundation rocks reeked of mold and moss. Lord, how she hated dark places, even more her disdain for eight legged creatures—and the horrid smell lingering made her retch.

Fear licked up her spine. What would she find down here? The letters she had read were terrifying. How could anyone live knowing that not only had her cousin abused her but that Edwin killed their parents? And to think the cad had made an advance while Benedict had been busy with the earl. Lord Cuthbert had no idea the mischief his son and nephew were up to.

She wondered if either of the disgusting men knew Helen had been with child. Could it truly have been her cousin's? Or, was it Gabriel's and that is why they were secretly engaged? Bile rose from the depths of her belly, making her nausea harder to deal with.

Estelle heard a conversation taking place, but she could not place what direction it came from.

The inspector had trailed behind to see if any new activities were going on in the manor. She had given him the direction on how to get to the cellar, and with any luck the man would be joining her soon.

She truly hoped that more officers would be following them here. Lord, if her parents knew she had snuck out, she knew not of what would happen. How she desired to see Benedict. Most emphatically, if something truly sinister was transpiring in there, they needed to get there without wasting further time.

When she had met with Ben's father, there was something about his demeanor when she mentioned that he might have gone missing at the earl's home; it had alarmed him. Estelle's intention of meeting with her future father-in-law had only been to gain a little insight into the Cuthbert's family history.

Estelle had not actually expected for the gentleman to already be in the company of the inspector. When Ben's father had explained that he had spent the majority of the last ten years hiding the earl's gambling trouble, and coordinating sales of properties in order to pay off debts, he began to uncover some unexpected truths. The man not only had a gambling problem, but whenever he had come into money, someone had mysteriously turned up dead, and money had once again slipped out of the coffers to silence another.

She had wondered how long it would be before someone caught on to the earl's schemes. The inspector had promised him to return his son alive and that he would bring justice to any wrong-doing. Although, he added, he would return for the earl's ledgers. If they played any role in any of his previous investigations, he would scrutinize each and every account.

Estelle heard that noise again as she moved closer and closer to it. The sound of a conversation sounded more like a plot to escape, but there was trouble. She tripped and fell to her knees, and that was when she found a barred-off room in the cellar. Not only did she take the humiliating tumble, she came face to face with Edwin, who looked more stunned than anything.

"Get out!" he cried out and stumbled back.

His action alerted his cellmate.

Her head throbbed from smacking it against the bars, and the stench nauseated her, but knowing she had found Ben imprisoned in the cellar made her swoon.

Estelle did not realize how much time had passed since she had fainted, but when she opened her eyes to find her beloved still bound, she cried. Estelle had found him and soon enough the inspector, and hopefully the constables, would find them and put this madness to rest.

"Sweetheart, you need to leave. George will be here anytime, and I promise you, he will be most displeased to find that you are here. He is a menacing fellow and will not hesitate to kill us all. Come on now, go."

Estelle blinked furiously into the darkness, thankful that he could not see the tears streaming down her face. *George is a menace, and so is his father. This whole family has a string of troubled minds. They should all be tried for their actions.*

"I cannot leave you, my love. The inspector is already here. It is only a matter of time before he finds us. If we die before that, it will be a comfort to know you have not died alone, and we will be together forever, as it should be."

"Quit speaking such nonsense, Estelle. You must leave." A gasp behind them alerted they were no longer alone.

"What in the world?"

Estelle turned around to find the countess standing there with her mouth gaping wide, and her hands trembling, making the lantern she held cast dancing shadows on the slime covered walls.

"You should not be here, Miss Humphrey. None of you should."

It was not until she walked closer did Estelle notice that Edwin's hand was bandaged. The countess had nearly dropped the lantern searching for a key at her waist to see if she could open the cell. A few minutes later, she fumbled with the lock and found the right one, opening it and permitting her entry.

"Help your fiancé up, Miss Humphrey, and be gone. The constables have arrived with the inspector from Scotland Yard. They're in the main house and an argument has ensued. I came in search of Edwin, as my son said that he was close, but so far out of reach. It was not until he said that did I notice what he meant. Now leave at once."

Estelle struggled to untie and lift her beloved from the floor, but the poor man moaned in pain. He had been beaten sorely and his breathing was heavy. Estelle turned back to see the countess cradling her nephew, who cried in her arms.

"My lady, have you known about this all along?"

"No." She choked back a sob. "I only found out this morning."

"You know what happened with Helen, too?"

The countess snorted and began to laugh manically. "That my son drugged her and had his way with her while she slept? I knew that she was planning on running off with that bastard Gabriel, too. She was planning on telling him what my son had done. I couldn't let her ruin my only child's life."

Horror slapped Estelle senseless until she recovered from the damning confession from Lady Cuthbert.

"You need to leave here at once." the countess hissed. "We're a damned lot. Every last one of us."

She kept walking and it was not until they reached near the exit that they heard the countess call out, "Forgive me, Lord, for all my transgressions. May Helen's soul rest in peace, and I hope that in her afterlife she can forgive me."

Two shots rang out behind them, and a sick feeling from the bottom of her stomach rose.

Estelle retched and released her fiancé, leaving him to drop as the bile rose up in her throat.

After a few more breaths, she returned to Ben, leading him out into the midafternoon sunlight. Servants came rushing at them, two of them taking Ben away from her.

"You must leave. The manor is ablaze and the constables have already taken the earl, and the inspector has run after Master George to the attic. There is an officer waiting to take you away, Miss. You should have never returned here."

Estelle sensed the urgency of the service staff and followed behind them. When they reached near the front of the manor where a carriage waited for them, the sound of glass shattering raised their attention.

Estelle looked up to find a body tumbling out of the window from the attic, and watched in horror as it landed with a thud several yards away.

The officer looked at her and whispered, "Wait here."

A servant shrieked. "It's the young Master George! Thank goodness that demonic fool is gone. The county can rest knowing he won't do harm to another living soul."

They were later joined by the lead inspector, who had just made it out in time. The manor had begun to collapse. Billows of smoke rose to the heavens. The house would take several hours before it completely reduced to rubble and ash.

A fitting end to an estate that became shadowed by sin.

Two months later…

E stelle packed hers and her husband's belongings with the aid of her maid and mother-in-law. She'd have never guessed in advance truly how much clutter could have been collected while they were abroad. Anxiously, she waited to hear back from Benedict, who'd left hours ago on a suspicious errand.

She ignored the way his mother ordered about the maid and the footmen from her own home, to aid them in their move to her first home as countess.

"Estelle, dear, while I am not accustomed to organize such a feat in small rooms as this, your assistance in taking charge would be appreciated. Not that I expect you've had any appropriate lessons. Now this is what I'd like you to do…"

Her sharp-tongued mother-in-law's words trailed off into silence as the door swung open and her husband appeared at the door.

Estelle rose to her feet, rushing over to him to embrace him. "What is it, dear? You were gone a very long time."

He turned to his mother and nodded. "Mama, I'd like a word in private with my wife."

"It's just as well; most of everything is ready to carry down to the carriage. I will return shortly."

"Come, sit down with me on the bed, dearest. I have much to say," Benedict instructed and she could do nothing but comply.

Her nerves began to get the best of her; from the dreaded fluttering of her belly, to her muscles tightening in her neck. *Heavens! Get over it, you silly girl.*

"I have just come back from the inspector's office. As it were, the Earl of Hawthorne has been charged with several counts of murder and illegal gambling, and interference with a criminal investigation. Considering the unfortunate suicide of his son, they had to turn the French investigators away, but not before learning of the terrible crimes George committed in his time abroad."

Estelle couldn't bear the thought of what sort of atrocities that man did in a foreign country, but could very well imagine how deviant and horrible they must have been.

"As it turns out, George had robbed people blind of their belongings, raped innocents, and if that weren't cruel enough, he was caught with a noble's wife. After being called out, he shot the man, returned to the wife only to brutally rape her before killing her too. The viscount's children hid while they watched their mama being attacked."

Benedict paused, pulling her into an embrace, shaking uncontrollably. Her husband—the love of her life—was upset which was quite natural given the circumstances of the horrors they experienced.

"I am truly sorry that we ever set foot in that house. I should have never asked you to attend with me, my love. I put you in danger and I'm a horrible person for doing so."

Estelle pushed away from his embrace to cup his cheeks. The sadness and hurt swimming in his eyes brought her to tears. "My love, there is nothing I would not have done for you. When we made the decision to attend the devil's party, it was under the premise to free your papa from whatever menacing hold that wretched family had on him."

She stopped to raise her hands and looked around, only to return her attention to him. "Look at us. We are alive; your family free from scandal and some very evil people have been stopped. If anything, we've rid society of some of England's worst scoundrels. I am glad we both came out of it alive. I do not think I would have been able to carry on if I lost you, my love."

Her tears fell uncontrollably now. This had been the first time since the events that they talked this freely and now they could carry on with their lives as they were meant to.

Benedict wiped the tears away and whispered, "Come, come. No more tears. We are free, have each other, and a lovely new home to enjoy in every aspect. I would love nothing more than to hear the pitter-patter of tiny feet. So let us leave the hotel in a pleasant mood, and let my mama enjoy ordering people about for just a second longer. I desire nothing more than to bless my countess with the loving she so deserves."

Estelle smiled and let the warmth of love wash over her like a warm sun shower. He was hers for eternity.

THE END

ABOUT THE AUTHOR

Born and raised in Toronto, Ontario, Layna discovered her love of reading at an early age. She's a bestselling author at All Romance eBooks, and multi-published author of historical, paranormal and contemporary erotic romances. When she isn't devouring salacious romance novels or writing, she enjoys losing herself in researching ancient history and mythology, weaponry, and hiking. She lives in Northern Ontario, with her husband and two daughters.

For updates on her upcoming releases, or to leave her a comment, you can find at:

Website: http://www.laynapimentel.com

OTHER TITLES BY THE AUTHOR